I was lying with my mouth full of dead leaves, shivering. I heard running feet, yells; an engine idled noisily down the block. I got my head up, then I got to my feet, took a couple of steps into deep shadow with feet that felt as though they'd been amputated and welded back on, badly. I stumbled again and fetched up against something scaled over with rust. I held on and blinked, made out the sweeping flank of m̲y̲ ... There was a cru... ...ining the dull b... ...med the rear ... ...eight grand on...

A foots... ...nd I suddenly remembered several things, none of them pleasant. I felt for my gun; it was gone. I moved back along the side of the car, stumbled, tried to hold on. No use. My arms were like unsuccessful pie crust. I slid down like a wet towel standing on end, lay among dead leaves; I sat up, listening to the steps coming closer. They stopped, and through a dense fog that had suddenly sprung up, I caught a glimpse of the tall white-haired figure standing over me. He had my pistol in his hand. He reached for me and then the fog closed in and swept everything away.

KEITH LAUMER

THE STARS MUST WAIT

BAEN BOOKS

THE STARS MUST WAIT

This is a work of fiction. All the characters and events portrayed in this book are fictional, and any resemblance to real people or incidents is purely coincidental.

A Baen Books Original

Baen Publishing Enterprises
260 Fifth Avenue
New York, N.Y. 10001

ISBN: 0-671-69859-1

Cover art by Larry Schwinger

First printing, February 1990

Distributed by
SIMON & SCHUSTER
1230 Avenue of the Americas
New York, N.Y. 10020

Printed in the United States of America

Prologue

It seemed like any other morning. Hell, it *was* like any other morning. Same heavy traffic outside the reservation; not ghouls out hoping to see death and destruction, just decent American citizens on the way to their jobs, with an idea they ought to be able to see *some*thing to look at outside a top secret NASA installation, on the day of the launch of *Prometheus,* man's first permanent colonizing effort on another world—in this case Callisto, as hospitable a world as was available. Jasperton hadn't been enthusiastic when NASA had decided to locate the *Prometheus* launch-site near their town— some rumors had circulated about the explosive potential of the ion drive and the energy sink. But they weren't hostile; after all, it had meant two hundred new jobs—and we needed to be where we were instead of in the Arizona desert, for logistical reasons. All there was to look at was the strip of well-manicured grass between the road and the chain-link fence, and the crisp sign beside the gate. The worried-looking recruit pulling guard duty gave an awkward salute. My return was equally uninspired.

One exception was the cluster of newshawks

just outside the gate under a cluster of TV cameras and lights. They waited until I was close to the gate and then closed in on me. I ran the window down; they had a right to know what was going to happen inside the closely-guarded site.

"Sir, you're Commander Jackson," a bland-faced fellow told me, peering in under the probing lenses.

"Gosh," I replied. "You must have peeked at my nameplate."

"No," he corrected lazily. "We know your car, sir. We've been waiting for you. You're the last of the crew to check in."

"Backup crew," it was my time to correct. "I'd have come sooner, but my orders say now."

He nodded, getting into my corner. "Sure, sir," he agreed this time. "Just how great is the danger of a megaton explosion when you light her off?"

"Nil," I told him.

"But the ion drive, Commander," he persisted. "According to this week's *Science News*, there's the potential to blast a crater bigger than Tycho. They say nobody knows the potential for disaster of this new drive."

"It's a regulation plasma particle accelerator," I told him. "All the reaction energy will be contained and dissipated by the energy sink." I started to move on, but he hung on and got red in the face.

"They say more energy than a hundred major lightning bolts," he gasped out.

I stopped the car and shook my head. He gave me a grateful look.

"That lightning can be tamed by a simple lightning rod," I reminded him. "The sink reduces the voltage, then dissipates it harmlessly into the bedrock."

"Why is a young man like yourself, a family man, willing to volunteer for a one-way mission like this?"

"The relief mission will be six months behind us. In six months we'll have the station operating and the relief crew can take over, and we'll come back."

"It seems strange, Commander," he persisted, "that all but one of both the primary and back-up crew members have small children. Couldn't they have found men without families for this risky mission?"

"Easily, but the computer that planned the mission wasn't concerned with humanitarian considerations; from the data the shrinks plugged into it, it computed that men with families would be most highly motivated to make a success of the mission and return home."

"Is there really much chance of that, sir?" he pressed me.

I nodded. "We're not suicidal. Our technology is the finest."

"But, Commander," he objected again, "a particle accelerator requires miles of travel; the smallest one in existence is a ring three miles in circumference!"

"We're using a spiral," I explained to him, "and we oscillate the particles, like AC. We got it down to half a mile that way; it's enough. The aft third of the vessel is devoted to the coil; the crew quarters are the center third; the fore section is filled with supplies—all we could possibly use, even if the relief is delayed and we're marooned for a couple of years."

"But Callisto is right here in the Solar System," he kept at his job. "Why is it necessary to use the matastasis—or easy sleep, as most people call it?"

"Nine years is too long for four men locked up in a coop," I told him. "The psychologists say in that time, we'd have forgotten what we were doing out there. Sounds nutty, but it's what we're up against. Nine years is the optimum orbit. It's not good, and no doubt better ways will be developed in the future, but for now, it's the best we can do: a nine-year passage, and a crew in stasis. It's not ideal from the human viewpoint, but the computer that worked it out didn't consider that."

"But—" he started. I was tired of the subject.

"We have the power to take the first real step to the stars, in our time," I told him. "We have to give it our best shot." I drove on, and he let it go at that. But his probing questions had upset me more than I was prepared to admit. Still, as I told him, I'd be home in time for dinner tomorrow, no worse for wear. We'd calculated the likelihood that any of the reserve crew would be called on in the final hours at .000 something.

"But, Commander," he was back objecting again, "Callisto is nothing but bare rock and ice and poison gas. How—"

"Our first move will be to make a few relatively minor adjustments to the drive to convert it to a ground-power unit," I told him. "With plenty of juice, we can extract oxygen from the rocks, burn hydrogen to make water, and synthesize material for the dome. It's made of a clear resin. We'll lay it out on a foundation, then inflate it. And there's no limit to how big we can make it as time goes by." I didn't tell him the rest: about how Callisto would become a new home for humanity, or about the super secret cargo of human and animal zygotes. Hell, *I* wasn't supposed to know about *that*. Maybe it was a crazy hope to make Callisto viable with a single mission, but right now NASA—and humanity—needed crazy hopes.

"Yes, very clever, I'm sure, sir," the newsman managed. "But as for yourself: Why is it you're to undergo the process of metastasis, I believe it's called? You'll be unconscious and immobilized for perhaps weeks, I understand. Why, when once the ship is away there'll be no need—"

"We're on stand-by, in case of any difficulty with the prime crew before lift-off. The process is not without its dangers, though it's been extensively tested. Jake Meyers did a full year with no problems. Still, problems *could* develop—we're walking a hairline between life and death, and rather than ship a corpse to Callisto, and then be shorthanded, it's better to be in a position to make a substitution, right up to the last moment."

"You're going in there, not knowing if you'll awaken in another world . . . or if you'll awaken at all," he said between breaths. "That's remarkable, Commander."

"Any military man is expected to be ready to do his job at the risk of his life if need be, at any time. Anyway, I expect to be out and home for dinner tomorrow at the latest. It's not so bad, so please don't dramatize it in your story and scare my wife to death."

"Still," he persisted, "there aren't many who'd volunteer for such an ordeal."

"There are eight of us," I reminded him. "That's a crew and a full back-up—all we need right now. And we happen to believe in the mission."

He gasped something more but I drove on. This time he let me go.

There was no activity on the ramp today. I pulled in beside MacGregor's worn-out brown Mercedes and went inside the Ops hut; some hut: twenty-two inches of pre-stressed composite over the service-tunnelhead. I went past Admin, skipped the lift, and took the long echoing walk down to the Pre-stage area. I heard voices down there, sounding a little louder than usual, but it was just old Bob's vid getting itself all worked up over the latest over-reaction: seems some hot-head had threatened to cut off aid to some lousy little pest-hole in the Middle East if they didn't stop murdering our diplomats. I felt a brief nostalgia for the good old days of round-the-clock thousand-plane strategic bombing.

Bob wasn't around; I went on along to Mac's office and stuck my nose around the jamb first, just in case he felt like shooting at something. I'd rather lose a nose than the whole head. No reaction. I went on in and said, " 'Don't you fellows *ever* bother to knock?' " to save him the trouble.

But my sardonic wit was wasted: this time, the office was empty. That was OK, I didn't really want to look at Mac's sour face. I went along, past Cargo and Technical to pers—pre-prep and harnessed up. The boys seemed a little jittery: Frank got my wires crossed and my right arm servo started jumping like a ten-day drunk. We got that fixed and he took his usual last look at me. His face looked tight and he kept poking his tongue out on his upper lip, as if to check if it was still there.

"What's biting you, MABE?" I asked him. That's "Middle-Aged Blue Eyes"—he hates looking like Sinatra used to, he says, even if he *was* named for him.

"Who, me?" he said, predictably. "I don't guess I'm taking it any harder than anybody else."

"Taking what?" I wanted to know. "The pay raise hasn't been shot down, has it?"

His face went as stiff as yesterday's pizza. "Under the circumstances, that's in pretty poor taste, Whiz, I think," he said, and looked at somebody else as if for confirmation.

"Gosh," I said, "I done up and insulted this here duchess, talking about money before breakfast. What circumstances?"

Now he looked at me again with a curious expression, as if I had a rarely-seen disease.

"You actually don't know, do you?" he asked me.

I shook my head. "Don't know what?" I came back on cue. "I've learned in life there's a number of things I don't know; which one did you have in mind?"

"Where've you been, Whiz?" he demanded.

"Fishing," I told him. "Timmy's birthday. I promised him last year we'd go and camp out. Great weekend."

"Didn't Ginny tell you?" he persisted. I told him I was getting tired of the game.

"Air Force One went down Friday, near Anchorage," he told me in a wooden voice. "The President and Veep were aboard, and General

Margrave. A Russian fighter out of Postov was sighted."

I felt the hackles standing up on the back of my neck. Really.

"Counter-strike?" I asked.

"Not yet," he admitted, as Mac came in. Nobody had anything else to say about it. I started to say something smart, but had sense enough to keep my mouth shut. Still, whatever gaiety the morning had had for me was gone.

We went on, past the vault-like service access doors into the final pre-staging section, the inner sanctum.

Final was a cramped little compartment adjacent to the personnel on-ramp to *Prometheus* herself, almost filled by the four stand-by cans. The other guys, Banner, Mallon, and Johnny, were already tucked in. I felt a little self-conscious about being the last man in. Of course, that meant I'd be the last man out, but I didn't care about that. I felt a throb of excitement, as it really hit me my next look at the sky might be from a dome on Callisto.

I barely felt the hyposprays that were feeding me the final catalysts that would activate all the stuff I'd been ingesting daily for the past six months. But of course I'd been this far before; it was only the possibility of waking up on a dead moon nine years from now that was different—a remote possibility. Nothing was going to go wrong with Day and his crew. Day and the others had been in their CEC's (that's Controlled-Environment Capsule) for seventy-two hours already and were set for another ten years, minimum. We reserve guys didn't know how long we'd be in this time, actually; maybe the full course, if there was unexpected trouble—unlikely. Our cans had been tested intensively for over five years. After we took off, it might be a week or two before they'd get around to cycling us out for the champagne launch party. At least that was what I'd told Ginny. I'd been in the can before, for as much as ten days; nothing to it; just a nice snooze on full pay and allowances.

"The mission is still go, of course?" was my next query. Surely we wouldn't fail *now*?

"Damn right," Mac supplied, having come up behind me. "Ten seconds behind schedule. Let's get you buttoned up here, Commander." He was doing his gruff efficiency number, like he always does when he's shook up, like when Ben fried in his can. That was the wrong thing for me to be thinking about while climbing into my own can and stretching out to wait for the base to be screwed down.

They took the usual readings, and closed me in. The damn coffin wasn't any cozier than usual, and the thought came to me that it was awful quiet in there. I felt as if I'd been maneuvered into a very costly and complicated trap, but what the hell: the pay raise was going through. This time next week I'd be making as much as a Manhattan garbage man.

I put all that out of my mind and tried to relax by the numbers. The can was as comfortable as the best brains in the business could make it. I caught just a whiff of the minty stuff and . . .

1

It *was* different this time: There was a dry pain in my lungs, and a deep ache in my bones, and a fire in my stomach that made me want to curl into a ball and mew like a kitten. My mouth tasted as though mice had nested in it, and when I took a deep breath, wooden knives twisted in my chest. I made a mental note to tell MacGregor a few things about his pet Controlled-Environment Capsule— just as soon as I got out of it.

It took a lot of effort to move a finger on the manual control console near my hand; there was a moment of delay; then somewhere in the distance a back-up unit whined: a faint whisper against total silence. The over-face panel glowed into life. Even that much light hurt my eyes; I had to squint to read the dials. Air pressure, temperature, G-field, humidity, CO_2 level, blood sugar, pulse and respiration and a lot of other stuff—A-OK. That was something. I flipped the intercom key and said, "OK, MacGregor, get me out of here. You've got problems . . ."

I had to stop to cough. The exertion made my temples pound, and I hurt all over.

"How long have you clowns run this damned

11

exercise?" I yelled, but it came out as a mumble. "I feel lousy," I told them. "What's going on around here? Why am I operating on back-up power?" Nothing happened.

No answer—and this was supposed to be the last run of the terminal test series. The boys couldn't all be out having coffee. The equipment had more bugs than a two-dollar hotel room, unless the totally unlikely had happened, and I was on Callisto. Negative. That G-reading showed good old Earth-normal. I touched the emergency release button. MacGregor wouldn't like it, but to hell with it! From the way I felt, I'd been in the tank for a good long stretch this time—maybe a week or two. And I'd told Ginny it would be a quick one—after all, *Prometheus* would be off in just a few hours—but maybe MacGregor had pulled a fast one on me. He might be a great technician, but he had no more human emotion than a loan officer. This time I'd tell him. . . .

Relays were clicking, equipment was retracting, air hissed, the tank cover slid back, I was sliding out. I sat up, swung my legs aside. It hurt. My muscles felt like King Tut's looked. The drugs and microspasm technique weren't working quite as advertised. I was shivering; it was cold. There was nobody in sight. I looked around at the dull gray walls, the data recording cabinets, the scarred wooden desk where Mac sat by the hour rerunning test profiles—and I saw three empty cans . . .

It was clear the launch had been aborted. The other CEC's were in disarray, their caps dangling from kinked wires—and empty. I yelled, "Hey,

Don!" No answer. "Johnny!" didn't work any better. "Let's face it," I told myself, "I'm alone down here."

Final pre-prep had never looked smaller. The board wasn't lit; that would be somebody's butt when Mac saw it, but I tried the back-up, and got green lights for Crew-Ready, Hull Integrity, Coil Idle, and Loading Complete. She was ready to go. Why hadn't she?

That was funny. The tape reels were empty and the red stand-by light was off. I stood, and felt dizzy. Where *was* Mac? Where were Banner and Johnny, and Mallon?

"Hey?" I called again, and didn't even get a good echo. *Some*one must have pushed the button to start my recovery cycle; where were they hiding now? I took a step, dragging the cables that trailed behind me. I unstrapped and pulled the harness off. The effort left me breathing hard. I opened one of the wall lockers: Day's pressure suit hung limply from the rack beside a rag-festooned coat-hanger. I looked in three more lockers. My clothes were missing—even my bathrobe. I also missed the usual bowl of hot soup, the happy faces of the aides, even Mac's sour puss.

It was cold and silent and empty here—more like a morgue than a top-priority research center. I didn't like it. What the hell was going on?

Then I got the big shock: the eight-inch-thick service-access door that opened on the tunnel leading to Power Section—the coil itself—was standing wide open. Not even visiting senators got to look in there. A rat ran out, unimpressed. I went in a few feet and saw litter on the floor, as if somebody had been working on his home-workshop project: bits of heavy cable, scraps of insulation, empty paper boxes with stock numbers. Ahead, I saw more of the same, plus a jury-rigged lighting system. This couldn't happen. I got out of there and took another look around Pre-Prep-Final, and Pre-Prep-Prelim. Supplies was still locked.

There was a second-hand-looking GI weather-suit in the last locker. I put it on, set the temperature control up to eighty, and felt some warmth begin to seep into my bones. I palmed the door open and stepped out into the lab proper. The Ultimate Top Secret access hatch leading up the ramp to *Prometheus*'s crew quarters stood shockingly ajar. No lights showed except for the dim glow of the emergency route indicators. There was trash scattered there, too. Someone had been tampering with *Prometheus*! That was unthinkable, so I didn't think it.

There was a faint, foul odor in the air. I heard a dry scuttling, and saw a flicker of movement. A rat the size of a fox squirrel sat up on his haunches six feet away, and looked up at me as if I were something to eat. I made a kicking motion and he ran off—but not very far. My heart was starting to thump a little harder now, the way it does when you begin to realize that something's *really* wrong this time—bad wrong. I had to find out how bad it was, somehow. I couldn't hide down here forever.

2

Upstairs, I peeked into Admin Section. Empty, of course. I called and coughed for a full minute; the echo was a little better here. I went along the corridor strewn with papers, past the open doors of silent rooms. In the director's office, a blackened wastebasket stood in the center of the rug. The air conditioner intake above the desk was felted over with matted black dust nearly an inch thick. There was no use shouting again; the place was as empty as a robbed grave—except for the rats. Even Bob's TV was gone.

At the end of the corridor, the inner security door stood open. I went through it and stumbled over something. In the faint light, it took me a moment to realize what it was. He had been an M.P., in steel helmet and riot boots. There was nothing left but crumbled bone and a few scraps of nibbled leather and some metal fittings. His nameplate was there: Levine. A .38 revolver lay nearby. I picked it up, checked the cylinder, and tucked it in the thigh pocket of the weather suit. For some reason, it made me feel a little better.

I went on along B corridor and found the galley. I ate a can of beans. They weren't very good, but they eased the burning a little. The lift door was sealed, but the emergency stairs were next to it. I started the two-hundred-foot climb to the surface. Coming down had been easier. I had to stop and rest twice, There was litter and dirt and rat droppings, and a few rat skeletons. Maybe things would look a little better up above—but I doubted it. If things were this bad here in the Inner Sanctum, they'd be worse elsewhere.

The heavy steel doors at the tunnel mouth had been blown clear—from the inside. Someone had been here, after the disaster, but ahead of me. I got through the half-blocked opening, looked out at a low gray sky burning red in the west. Fifty yards away, the five-thousand-gallon water tank lay in a tangle of rusty steel. What had it been? Sabotage, war, revolution—an accident? And where *was* everybody? I had another coughing fit.

I rested for a while, then went across to the tank and climbed twenty feet up the broken steelwork to look out across the innocent-looking—but weed-covered—fields to the west, dotted with the dummy buildings that were supposed to make the site look from the air like the stretch of farmland it had been before Operation *Prometheus* came along. It was complete with barns, sheds, and fences. The parking lot was empty, except for two rusty Hondas locked in collision; that made me remember the real world—Ginny—and Timmy.

The turnpike lights were off, and where the glow of the big city fifty miles away should have been, there were only a few scattered lights. I almost slipped coming around fast to look north toward Jasperton; the sound I made was more a whimper than anything else—

Beyond the site, the town seemed to be intact: there were dim yellow lights twinkling here and there, a few smudges of smoke rising. Whatever had happened at the site, at least Ginny would be all right—Ginny and Tim. Ginny would be worried sick, after—how long? A month? Maybe more. There hadn't been much left of that Marine.

I twisted right to get a view of the south, and felt a hollow sensation in my chest. Two silo doors stood open; the Colossus missles had hit back—at something. I pulled myself up a foot or two higher for a look at the Primary Site. In the twilight, the ground rolled smooth and unbroken across the spot where *Prometheus* lay ready in her underground berth. There was a string of modest, sub-N craters across the area, but down below she was safe and sound according to the back-up readout. She had been built to stand up to the stresses of a direct extra-solar-orbital launch; with any luck, a few near-misses wouldn't have damaged her. Far beyond, above the trees, the top of the new Hilton Suburban was visible, lit up all the way to the penthouse. That was something. I knew where I was heading now.

My arms were aching from the strain of holding on. I was out of shape, but I seemed to be recovering fast. Maybe the treatment wasn't entirely useless. I climbed down, sat on the ground to get my breath, watching the cold wind worry the dry stalks of dead brush around the fallen tank. It was obvious there'd been some kind of disaster, maybe a short war over the loss of Air Force One. At home Ginny and Timmy would be alone, scared, maybe even in serious difficulty. There was no telling how far municipal services had broken down.

But before I headed that way, I'd make a quick check on the ship. *Prometheus* was a dream that I—and a lot of others—had lived with for ten years. I'd seen the evidence of tampering; I wanted to be reassured. I headed toward the pillbox that housed the tunnel head on the off-chance that a usable car might be parked over there; it would be a long walk home for a sick man.

It was almost dark and the going was tough; the reinforced concrete slabs under the sod were tilted and dislocated. Something had sent a ripple across the ground like a stone tossed into a pond. I heard a sound and stopped dead. There was a *clank!* and a rumble from beyond the discolored walls of the blockhouse a hundred yards away. Rusted metal howled; then something as big as a beached freighter moved into view. Two dull red beams stabbed out from near the top of the high silhouette; they swung, flashed crimson and held. The siren went off—an ear-splitting *whoop! whoop!* It was the unmanned Bolo Mark II Combat Unit on auto-mated sentry duty—and its intruder-sensing cir-cuits were tracking me.

The Bolo pivoted heavily. The *whoop! whoop!* sounded again; the robot watchdog was bellowing the alarm. I felt sweat pop out on my forehead, and I was suddenly aware of the weight of the canned beans. My electropass was back in the shop, and standing up to a Mark II Bolo without it was the rough equivalent of being penned in with an ill-tempered dinosaur. I looked toward the primary block-house: too far. The same went for the perimeter fence. My best bet was back to the service-tunnel mouth. I turned to sprint for it, hooked a foot on a slab and went down hard . . .

I sat up. My head was ringing, and I tasted blood in my mouth. The chipped pavement seemed to rock under me. The Bolo was coming up fast. Running was no good; I had to have a better idea.

I dropped flat, switched my suit control to maximum insulation; the silvery surface faded to dull black. A few inches away a two-foot square of tattered paper fluttered against a projecting edge of concrete. I reached for it, peeled it free, then fumbled with a pocket flap, brought out a permatch, flicked it alight. When the paper was burning well, I tossed it clear. The wind whirled it away a few feet, then it caught in a clump of grass. The Bolo would track a moving IR source.

"Keep moving, damn you!" I hissed. The swearing worked. The gusty wind pushed the paper on. I crawled a few feet, squeezed into a crack between slabs. The Bolo churned closer; a loose tread-plate was slapping the earth with a rythmic thudding. The burning paper was fifty feet away now, almost gone, a twinkle of orange light in the deep twilight. Keep burning, damn you!

At twenty yards, looming like a pagoda, the Bolo halted, sat rumbling, swivelling its rust-streaked turret, looking for the moving heat source its IR had sensed momentarily. The feeble flare of the paper finally caught its electronic attention; it must be as sick as I was. The turret swung, then back. It was puzzled. It *whoop!*ed again, then reached a decision: gun-ports snapped open; a vol-

ley of anti-personnel slugs *whoof!*ed, and the scrap
of paper disappeared in a gout of tossed dirt.

I hugged the ground like gold lamé hugs a torch
singer's hip and waited; nothing happened. The
Bolo sat, rumbling softly to itself. This went on for
a long time. Then I heard another sound over the
murmur of the idling engine—a distant roaring,
like a flight of low-level bombers. I raised my head
half an inch and took a look. There were lights
moving on the highway to the north—the paired
beams of a convoy approaching from town. The
Bolo's activity hadn't passed unnoticed.

The Bolo stirred, moved heavily forward until it
towered over me no more than twenty feet away. I
saw the big gun-ports open, high up on the armored facade—the ones that housed the heavy
infinite repeaters. The tips of slim black muzzles
slid into view, hunted for an instant, then de-
pressed, and locked—bearing on the oncoming
vehicles, which were spreading out now along the
road beyond the fence in a loose skirmish line
under a roiling layer of dust.

The watchdog was getting ready to defend its
territory—and I was caught in the middle. A blue-
white flood-light lanced out from the convoy, glared
against the scaled plating of the Bolo. I heard
relays *click!* inside the monster fighting machine,
and braced myself for the thunder of her battery. . . .

There was a dry rattle. The guns traversed,
clattering emptily. From beyond the fence the
floodlight played for a moment longer against the
Bolo, then moved on across the ramp, back, across
and back, searching . . . for *me*. I made myself as
flat as a cockroach easing under a door.

Once more the Bolo fired its empty guns. Its red IR beams swept the scene again; then relays snicked, the impotent guns retracted, the port covers closed. Satisfied it had done its job, the Bolo heaved itself around, moved off, trailing a stink of ozone and ether, the broken tread thumping like a cripple on a stair.

I was getting awfully warm in the sealed suit, but I waited until the Bolo had disappeared in the gloom a couple of hundred yards away; then I cautiously turned my suit control to vent off the heat. Full insulation would boil a man in his own gravy in less than half an hour. The floodlight had blinked off now. I got to my hands and knees and started toward the perimeter fence, off to the left. The Bolo's circuits weren't tuned as fine as they should have been; it let me go.

3

There were men moving in the glare and dust beyond the remains of the rusty lacework that had once been a chain-link security fence. They carried odd-looking rifles and stood in tight little groups, staring across toward the blockhouse. I moved closer, keeping flat and avoiding the avenues of yellowish light thrown by the headlamps of the parked vehicles—half-tracks, armored cars, a few light manned tanks. There was nothing about the look of this crowd that impelled me to leap up to be welcomed. Some of them were wearing green uniforms, or pieces of them, and most of them sported full beards. What the hell? Had Castro II landed in force?

I angled off to the right, away from the big main gate that had been manned day and night by guards with M-100s; it hung now by one hinge from a scarred concrete pier under a cluster of dead polyarcs in corroded brackets. The sign that had read NASA—GLENN AEROSPACE CENTER—AUTHORIZED PERSONNEL ONLY lay face down in hip-high underbrush.

More cars were coming, crowding in close to the main gate. Men piled out; they seemed disorganized. There was a lot of talking and shouting: a squad formed up raggedly, and headed my way, keeping to the outside of the fallen fence, but they couldn't see me. I was outside the glare of the lights now; I chanced a run for it, got over the sagged wire and across the potholed blacktop of State Road 35 and into the ditch well ahead of them. The detail dropped men in pairs at fifty-yard intervals. I had gotten out barely in time; another five minutes and they would have intercepted me—along with whatever else they were after.

I worked my way back across an empty lot, into a strip of lesser underbrush that Mac had always been going to get cleared. It was lined with shaggy trees that seemed bigger than I remembered. Beneath them patches of cracked sidewalk showed here and there.

Several things were beginning to be a little clearer now: the person who had pushed the button to bring me out of stasis hadn't been around to greet me—because no one had pushed it. The automatics, triggered by some malfunction, had initiated the emergency recovery cycle. The system's self-contained power unit had been designed to maintain a starship crewman's minimal vital functions indefinitely at reduced body temperature and metabolic rate. There was no way to tell exactly how long I had been in the tank; from the condition of the fence and the roads, it had been more than a matter of weeks—or even months. Had it been a year . . . or more? I thought of Ginny and the boy, waiting at home, thinking the old man was dead, probably. I'd neglected them before for my work, but not like this. . . .

Our house was six miles from the base, in the foothills on the other side of town. It was a long walk, the way I felt—but I had to get there. . . .

4

Two hours later, I was clear of the town, following the river bank north. I kept having the idea that someone was following me, but when I stopped to listen, there was never anything there; just the still, cold night, and the frogs, singing away patiently in the low ground off to the right.

When the ground began to rise, I left the road, struck off across the open fields. I reached a side street, followed it in a curve that would bring me out at the foot of Ridge Avenue—my street. I could make out the shapes of the low, rambling houses now. It had been the kind of residential section the local Junior Chamber members had hoped to move into some day. Now the starlight that filtered through the cloud cover showed me broken windows, doors that sagged open, automobiles that squatted on flat, dead tires under collapsing car shelters—and here and there a blackened, weed-grown foundation, like a gap in a row of rotting teeth. There were no lights showing in the houses. The neighborhood wasn't what it had been; how long had I been away? How long . . .?

Something went *crack!* behind me. I hit the dirt, hard this time. I listened: nothing. It wasn't

27

easy getting up. I seemed to weigh a hell of a lot
for a guy who hadn't been eating regularly. My
breathing was fast and shallow, and my skull was
getting ready to split and give birth to a live
alligator—the ill-tempered kind. It was only a few
hundred yards more; but why the hell had I picked
a house halfway up a hill?

I heard the sound again—a crackle of dry grass.
I got the pistol out and stood flat-footed in the
middle of the street, listening hard. All I heard
was my stomach growling. I took the pistol off
cock and started off again, stopped suddenly a
couple of times to catch him off-guard; nothing. I
reached the corner of Ridge Avenue, started up
the slope. Behind me, a stick popped loudly. I
picked that moment to fall down again. Heaped
leaves saved me from another skinned knee. I
rolled over against a low fieldstone wall, propped
myself against it; I had to use both hands to cock
the pistol. I stared into the dark, but all I could
see were the little lights whirling again. The pistol
got heavy; I put it down, concentrated on taking
deep breaths and blinking away the fireflies. I
heard footsteps plainly, close by; he didn't care,
now. I shook my head, accidently banged it against
the stone wall behind me. That helped. I saw him,
not over twenty feet away, coming up the hill
toward me, a big, black-haired man with a full
beard, dressed in odds and ends of rags and furs,
gripping a polished length of knobbed wood with a
leather thong looped in one end. I reached for the
pistol, found only leaves, tried again, touched the
butt and knocked it away.

I was still groping when I heard a scuffle of feet.

I swung around, saw a second man, a tall, wide figure with a mass of untrimmed white hair. He hit the bearded man like a pro tackle taking out the practice dummy, and they went down together hard, rolled over in a flurry of dry leaves. The cats were fighting over the mouse; that was my signal to leave quietly. I made one last grab for the gun, found it, got to my feet and staggered off up the grade that seemed as steep now as penthouse rent.

And from downslope, I heard an engine gunned, the clash of a heavy transmission that needed adjustment. A spotlight fickered on, made shadows dance. I could tell who was winning the fight; it didn't matter anyway.

I recognized a fancy wrought-iron fence with some of the iron spears missing, fronting a vacant lot: that had been the Adams house. Only half a block to go—but I was losing my grip fast. I went down twice more, then gave up and started crawling. I could hear the tussle still going on behind me. My head split open, dropped off, and rolled down-hill. Just a few more yards to go now and I could let it all go. Ginny would put me in a warm bed, patch up my scratches, and feed me soup. Ginny would . . . Ginny . . .

5

I was lying with my mouth full of dead leaves, shivering. I heard running feet, yells; an engine idled noisily down the block. I got my head up, found myself looking at chipped brickwork and the heavy wrought-iron hinges from which my front gate had hung. The gate was gone and there was a large chunk of brick missing. Maybe it wasn't battle damage; some delivery truck had just missed his approach.

I got to my feet, took a couple of steps into deep shadow with feet that felt as though they'd been amputated and welded back on, badly. I stumbled again and fetched up against something scaled over with rust. I held on and blinked, made out the sweeping flank of my brand new '01 Firebird. There was a crumbled crust of whitish glass lining the dull brightwork strip that had framed the rear window. And I still owed eight grand on it!

A footstep sounded behind me, and I suddenly remembered several things, none of them pleasant. I felt for my gun; it was gone. I moved back along the side of the car, stumbled, tried to hold on. No use. My arms were like unsuccessful pie crust. I slid down like a wet towel standing on end, lay among dead leaves; I sat up, listening to the steps coming closer. They stopped, and through a dense fog that had suddenly sprung up, I caught a glimpse of the tall white-haired figure standing over me. He had my pistol in his hand. He reached for me and then the fog closed in and swept everything away.

6

I was lying on my back this time, on a heap of dampish rags, looking across at the smoky yellow light of a thick brown candle guttering in the draft from a window with no glass. In the center of the room, a few sticks of damp-looking wood heaped on a patch of cracked asphalt tiles rimmed with charred wall-to-wall burned with a grayish flame. The fire sent a thin curl of acrid smoke up to stir the cobwebs festooned under ceiling beams from which the wood veneer had peeled away to reveal the light-alloy trusswork beneath. It was a strange scene, but not so strange that I didn't recognize it: it was my own living room—looking a little different from when I had seen it last. The odors were different, too; I picked out mildew, badly-cured leather, damp wool, fecal matter, tobacco . . .

I turned my head, not without effort. A yard from the rags I lay on, the white-haired man sat sleeping with his back against the wall, looking older than Pharaoh. My Webley ten-gauge was gripped in one big, gnarled hand, and his head was tilted back, his blue-veined eyelids shut. Caked blood was black in his hair. I sat up; at my movement, his eyes opened. He lay relaxed for a moment, as though life had to return from some-place far away; then he raised his hand, and I got set for the blow, but instead he gave me an awkward salute. His face was hollow and deep-lined, his white hair thin. A coarse-woven shirt hung loose across wide shoulders that had been Herculean once—but now Hercules was old, old. . . . He looked down at me expectantly for a long moment.

"Who are you?" I asked him. My long-unused voice was a croak, and I had to cough some more. "Why did you follow me?" I asked, when I could breathe again. "What happened to the house? Where's my family? Who owns the bully-boys in green? What do they want with me?" My jaw hurt when I spoke. I put my hand up and felt it gingerly. My whiskers were a quarter of an inch long. "Who were you fighting with?" I threw in for good measure.

"You fell," the old man said, in a voice that rumbled like a subterranean volcano.

"The understatement of the year, Pop," I said without coughing. I tried to get up. Nausea knotted my stomach.

"You must rest," the old man said, looking concerned, "before the Baron's men come again . . ." He paused, looking at me as though he expected me to say something profound.

"I want to know where the people are that live here . . ." My yell came out as weak as church-social punch. "A woman and a boy . . ." More coughing. I decided to save my throat for regular breathing.

He was shaking his head. "You have to do something quickly," he told me soberly. "The soldiers will come back, search every house—"

I sat up, ignoring the little men driving spikes into my skull. "I don't give a damn about soldiers!" I told Pop. "Where's my family? What's happened?" I reached out and gripped his bony arm. "How long was I down there? What year is this?"

He only shook his head. "Come, eat some prime. Then I can help you with your plan."

It was no use talking to the old man; he seemed to assume that I'd fix everything, but then he was senile. I got off the floor; except for the dizziness and a feeling that my knees were made of wet papier maché, I was all right. I picked up the hand-formed candle, stumbled through, pushed open the door to my study. There was my desk, the tall bookcase with the glass door, the gray rug, the easy chair. Aside from a half-inch layer of dust and some peeling wallpaper, it looked almost normal. I flipped the wall switch. Nothing happened.

"What is that charm?" the old man said behind me. He was pointing to the switch.

"The power's off," I said. "Just habit."

He reached out and flipped the switch up, then down again "It makes a pleasing sound," he said, sounding pleased.

"Yeah." I picked up a book from the desk; it fell apart in my hands.

I dropped it in the wastebasket, went back into the hall, tried the guestroom door, looked in at heaped leaves, the remains of broken furniture, an empty window frame. I went on to the end of the hall, into the master bedroom.

A cold night wind blew through a barricade of broken timbers. The roof had fallen in, and a twelve-inch tree-trunk slanted through the wreckage. The old man stood behind me, watching.

"Where is she, damn you?" I snarled, and coughed some more. I leaned against the door frame to swear and fight off the faintness. "Where's my wife . . . ?" I demanded, but the old man just looked troubled.

"Come, eat now . . ." he said.

"Where is she?" I kept after him. He was my only source of information; he *had* to answer. "Where's the woman who lived here?"

He frowned, shook his head dumbly. I picked my way through the wreckage, stepped out through broken bricks into knee-high brush and cold wind. A gust blew my candle out. In the dark I stared at my back yard, the crumbled pit that had been a barbecue grill, the tangled thickets that had been rose beds—and a weathered length of board upended in the earth. "What the hell's this . . . ?" I fumbled out a permatch, lit my candle, leaned close and read the crude letters cut into the crumbling wood:

VIRGINIA ANNE JACKSON.
BORN JAN 8, 1965.
KILL BY THE DOGS, WINTER 1992.

7

The Baron's men came twice in the next three days, and each time the old man saw them coming and carried me, swearing plenty but too weak to resist, out to a lean-to of branches and canvas in the woods behind the house; then he disappeared, to come back an hour or two later and haul me back to my rag bed by the fire.

Three times a day he gave me a tin pan of stew that he got out of cans, and I ate it mechanically. My mind went over and over the picture of Ginny, living on for a year in the slowly decaying house, and then . . .

It was too much. There are some shocks the mind refuses. I thought of the tree that had fallen and crushed the east wing; an elm that size was at least fifty to sixty years old—maybe older. And the only elm on the place had been a two-year sapling. I knew it well; I had planted it myself.

My contemporaries, Mac and even all the young techs—they were all dead of old age, long ago. How had they died? But the fellows aboard ship—they'd still be there, waiting. . . .

The old man was too far gone to tell me anything useful; most of my questions produced a shake of the head and a few mumbled words about charms, demons, spells, the Baron.

"I don't believe in spells," I said. "And I'm not too sure I believe in this Baron. Who is he?"

"The Baron of Philly; he holds all this country—" The old man made a sweeping gesture with his arm. "All the way to Jersey."

"Why is he looking for me? What makes me important?"

"You came from the Forbidden Place," Pop told me impassively. "Everyone heard the cries of the Lesser Troll that stands guard over the treasure there. If the Baron can learn your secrets of power—"

"Troll, hell! That's nothing but a Bolo on automatic!"

"By any name every man dreads the monster, scarce less than the Noocler itself. A man who walked in its shadow is one to dread indeed. But the others—the ones that run in a pack like dogs— would tear you to pieces for a demon if they could lay hands on you."

"You saw me back there; why didn't you give me away? Why did you help me? And why are you taking care of me now?"

He shook his head—the all-purpose reply to any question he didn't want to answer. I tried another angle: "Who was the rag man you tackled just outside? Why was he laying for me?"

The old man snorted. "Tonight the dogs will eat

him. But forget that. Now we have to talk about your plan—"

"I've got about as many plans as the senior boarder in Death Row," I told him. "I don't know if you know it, Old Timer, but somebody slid the world out from under me while I wasn't looking—"

The old man frowned. I had the thought that I wouldn't like to have him mad at me, for all his white hair. . . .

He shook his head. "You must understand what I tell you," he said seriously. "The men of the Baron will find you at last; but if you are to break the spell—"

"Break the spell, eh?" I snorted. "I think I get the idea, Pop: You've got it in your head that I'm a valuable property of some kind. You figure I can use my supernatural powers to take over this menagerie and you'll be in on the ground floor. Well, listen, you old fool: I spent the best part of a century—maybe more—in a stasis tank two hundred feet underground. My world died while I was down there. This Baron of yours seems to own everything now. If you think I'm going to get myself shot bucking him, forget it!"

The old man didn't say anything; he just looked at me expectantly.

"Things don't seem to be broken up much," I went on, explaining to myself. "It must have been gas, or germ warfare—or fallout. Damn few people around. You're still able to live on what you can loot from stores; automobiles are still sitting where they were the day the world ended. How old were you when it happened, Pop? The war, I mean. Do you remember it?"

He shook his head. "The world has always been as it is now."

"What year were you born?"

He scratched at his white hair. "I knew the number once—but I've forgotten."

"I guess the only way I'll find out exactly how long I was gone is to saw that damned elm in two and count the rings," I told him—or myself. "But even that wouldn't help much, I don't know when it blew over. Never mind. The important thing now is to talk to this Baron of yours. Where does he stay? How do I get an appointment with him?"

The old man shook his head violently. "If the Baron lays his hands on you, he'll wring the secrets from you on the rack! I know his ways. For five years I was a slave in the palace garages—"

"If you think I'm going to spend the rest of my days in this rat nest, you get another guess on the house," I told him. "This Baron has tanks, an army. He's kept a little technology alive. That's the outfit for me—not this garbage detail. Now, where's this palace of his located?"

"The guards will shoot you on sight like a packdog!"

"There has to be a way to get to him, old man! Think!"

The old man was shaking his head again. "He fears assassination. You can never approach him . . ." He brightened. "Unless you know a spell of power . . . ?"

I chewed my lip. "Maybe I do at that. You wanted me to have a plan. I think I feel one coming on. Have you got a map?" He pointed to the desk beside me. I tried the drawers, found mummified mice, roaches, moldy money—and a stack of folded roadmaps. I remembered putting them there last week. Some week. I opened one carefully: faded ink on yellowed paper, falling apart at the creases. The legend in the corner read: PENNSYLVANIA 40M:1. Copyright 2011 by Exxon Corporation.

"This will do, Pop," I said. "Now, tell me all you can about this Baron."

"You'll destroy him?"

"I haven't even met the man."

"He is evil."

"I don't know; he owns an army. That makes up for a lot . . ."

8

After three more days of rest and Pop's stew, I was back to normal—or near enough. I had the old man boil me a tub of water for a bath and a shave. I found a serviceable pair of synthetic-fiber longjohns in a chest of drawers, pulled them on and zipped the weather suit over them, then buckled on the holster I had made from the bottom of a tough plastic garment bag.

"That completes my preparations, Pop," I said. "It'll be dark in another half hour. Thanks for everything."

He got to his feet. There was a worried look on his lined face, like a father the first time Junior asks for the car.

"The Baron's men are everywhere," he told me, but he went on to disclose that one night a week there was a big shindig at the Palace, and tonight was the night. "If you must go, this is the best time," he agreed with himself, nodding.

"If you want to help me, come along and back me up with that shotgun of yours," I said. I picked it up. It was worn but not rusted; he'd taken good care of it. "Have you got any shells for this thing?" I asked him.

He smiled, pleased now. "There are shells—but the magic is gone from many."

"That's the way magic is, Pop. It goes out of things before you notice."

"Will you destroy the Great Troll now?"

"My motto is let sleeping trolls lie. I'm just paying a social call on the Baron."

The joy ran out of his face like booze from a dropped jug.

"Don't take it so hard, Old Timer," I suggested. "I'm not the fairy prince you were expecting—but I'll take care of you—if I make it."

I waited while he pulled on a moldy-looking mackinaw with only one sleeve. He took the shotgun and checked the breech, then looked at me.

"I am ready," he said.

"Yeah," I said. "Let's go . . ."

9

It was a five-mile trek through deserted streets and a cracked-up highway, dodging greenbacks all the way—I didn't see anybody else abroad on the pitted road or the overgrown fields—to the baronial palace, a forty-story slab of concrete and glass that had been known in my day as the Hilton Suburban. We made it in three hours, at the end of which I was puffing but still on my feet. We moved out from the cover of the trees and looked across a dip in the ground at the lights, incongruously cheerful in the ravaged valley. There was no activity here.

"The gates are there—" the old man pointed— "guarded by the Great Troll."

"Wait a minute; I thought the Troll was the Bolo back at the Site."

"That is the Lesser Troll. This is the Great One—"

I selected a few choice words and muttered them to myself. Aloud I said, "It would have saved us some effort if you'd mentioned this Troll a little sooner, Old Timer. I'm afraid I don't have any spells that will knock out a Mark II, once it's got its dander up."

He shook his head. "It lies under enchantment. I remember the day long ago, when it came, throwing thunderbolts. All men fled from it. Then the Baron commanded it to stand at his gates to guard him—"

"How long ago was this, Old Timer?"

He worked his lips over the question. "Long ago," he said finally. "Many winters. I was young and strong then."

"Let's go take a look."

We picked our way down the slope, came up along a rutted dirt road to the dark line of trees that rimmed the palace grounds. The old man touched my arm.

"Softly here. They say the Great Troll sleeps lightly . . ."

I went the last few yards, eased around a brick pier beside a blocked gateway with a dead lantern on top, stared across a few hundred yards of waist-high brush at a dark silhouette looming against the palace lights. Cables between the trees supported a weathered tarp which drooped over the Bolo. The wreckage of a helicopter lay like a crumpled dragonfly at the far side of the disc of light. Nearer, fragments of a heavy car chassis lay scattered. The old man hovered at my shoulder.

"It looks as though the gate's off limits," I hissed. "Let's try farther along."

He nodded. "No one passes here," he whispered. "There is a second gate, there—" He pointed to the left. "But there are lights, and many guards."

"We'll have to climb the wall between the gates," I suggested.

"There are sharp spikes on the top of the wall,"

he told me, "but I know a place, farther on, where the spikes have been blunted—"

"Lead on, Pop."

Half an hour of creeping through wet brush brought us to the spot Pop said we were looking for. It looked to me like any other stretch of eight-foot masonry wall overhung with wet poplar trees.

"I will go first," the old man said, "to draw the attention of the guard."

"Then who's going to boost me up?" I objected. "I'll go first."

He nodded, cupped his hands; I stepped in, and he lifted me as easily as a sailor lifting a beer glass. Pop was old, but he was nobody's softie.

I looked around, then crawled up, worked my way over the corroded spikes, dropped down on the lawn. Immediately, I heard a crackle of brush. A man stood up, not twenty feet away, cradling a wicked-looking weapon. I lay flat in the dark, trying to look like something that had been there a long time. . . .

I heard another sound, from up ahead: a *thump!* and a crashing of brush. The guard moved off, and quickly disappeared in the darkness. I heard him beating his way through the shrubbery; then he called out, and got an answering shout from the distance. The old man was keeping them distracted. I hoped he was OK, but I didn't loiter. I got to my feet and made a sprint for the cover of the trees along the drive.

10

In total darkness, I lay flat on the wet ground under the wind-whipped branches of an ornamental cedar, blinking a fine misty rain from my eyes, smelling the piney odor, waiting for the half-hearted alarm behind me to die down. There were a few shouts, some sounds of searching among the shrubbery, but it was a bad night to be chasing imaginary intruders in the Baronial grounds, and in five minutes all was quiet again. Pop didn't show, but I told myself he'd stuck longer than I had any right to expect.

I studied the view before me. The tree looming over me was one of a row lining the drive that swung in a graceful curve across a smooth quarter-mile of the dark lawn to the tower of light that was the palace of the Baron of Philly. The silhouetted figures of guards and late-arriving guests moved against the gleam from the collonaded entrance. On a terrace high above, dancers twirled under colored lights in the faint glow of the repeller field that kept the cold rain at a distance. In a lull in the wind, I heard music, faintly. Pop had told me the Baron's weekly Grand Ball would be in full swing by this time.

I saw shadows move across the wet gravel in front of me; then I heard the purr of an engine. I hugged the ground and watched a long svelte Mercedes—a 20-something model, I estimated— barrel past. The driveway was almost smooth. Like the state road to the site, its potholes had been patched with rammed pebbles. The mob in the countryside ran in packs like dogs, but the Baron's friends did a little better for themselves. Even so, there weren't many cars here; most of the guests arrived on foot in spite of the weather.

I got to my feet, not without stifling a few groans, and moved off toward the palace-hotel, keeping well in the shadows. Where the drive swung to the right to curve across in front of the building, I left it, went to hands and knees, and followed a trimmed privet hedge past dark rectangles of formal garden to the edge of the secondary pond of light from the garages. I tucked in behind the nearest clump of flowering arbutus and let myself down on my belly to watch the shadows that moved on the wet blacktop drive. There seemed to be two men on duty, no more. Waiting around wouldn't improve my chances. I got to my feet, stepped out onto the pavement, and walked openly around the corner of the grey fieldstone building into the light.

I remembered, incongruously, the last time I'd seen the place: the Grand Opening Ball, with Ginny looking so lovely in her pea-green velvet that fit her like her own hide, and no harness under it to break those beautiful curves, and me looking pretty sharp in the white mess jacket with the fancy shoulderboards.

Where the big copper letters had been, there were ghostly outlines and broken rivets, reading ILTO UB RB.

I said, "Yeah, 'ilto ub rb' to you, too," and eased forward another few yards, trying to look bored as the men turned to look at me. A short, thick-set fellow in greasy baronial green looked me over incuriously. My weather-suit looked enough like ordinary coveralls to get me by—at least for a few seconds, I hoped. Another man, tilted back against the wall in a wooden chair, didn't even turn his head.

"Hey!" I called. "You birds got a three-ton jack I can borrow?"

Shorty looked me over sourly. "Who you drive for, Mac?"

"The High Duke of Jersey," I improvised. "Lost gauss, left rear. On a night like this. Some luck."

"The Jersey can't afford a jack?" Shorty grunted.

I stepped over to him, prodded him with a forefinger. "He could buy you and gut you on the altar any Saturday night of the week, Low-pockets," I growled at him. "And he'd get a kick out of doing it. He's like that."

"Can't a guy crack a harmless gag without somebody talks about altar-bait?" he protested. "You wanna jack, take a jack."

The man in the chair opened one eye and looked me over. "How long you on the Jersey payroll?"

"Long enough to know who handles the rank between Jersey and Philly," I told him and yawned. I looked around the wide, concrete-floored garage, glancing over the four heavy cars with the Philly crest on their sides. "Where's the kitchen?" I demanded. Politeness would be misunderstood by these boys. "I'm putting a couple of hot coffees under my belt before I go back out into that."

"Over there." Low-pockets pointed. "A flight up and to your left. Tell the cook Pintsy invited you—"

"I'll tell him Jersey sent me, Junior." I moved off in a dead silence, opened the door and stepped up into spicy-scented warmth. A deep carpet—even here—muffled my footsteps. I could hear the clash of pots and crockery from the kitchens a hundred feet or so along the hallway. I went along to a deep-set doorway ten feet from the kitchen suite, tried the knob, looked into a dark storeroom. I shut the door, leaned against it, and watched the kitchen doors, smelling smells that made my jaws ache: roast fowl, baked ham, grilled chops . . . Through the woodwork I could feel the thump of the bass notes from the orchestra blasting away three flights up. There was a small door off to the right, probably for putting the garbage out. I went over and slid back the barrel-bolt.

Five slow minutes passed. Then the kitchen door swung open down the hall, and a tall, round-shouldered fellow in black livery, with a shiny bald scalp and a modest little paunch, stepped into view, a tray balanced on the spread fingers of one hand. He turned, the black tails of his cutaway swirling, called something behind him, and started toward the niche I was concealed in. I waited until he'd passed, then stepped out and cleared my throat. He shied, whirled to face me. He was good at his job: the two dozen tiny glasses on the tray stood fast. He blinked, got an indignant remark ready—

I showed him the knife the old man had lent me—a bone-handled job with a six-inch blade. "Make a sound and I'll cut your throat," I said softly. "Put the tray on the floor."

He started to back away; I brought the knife up. He took a good look at it, licked his lips, then crouched quickly and put the tray down.

"Turn around."

I stepped in and chopped him at the base of the neck with the edge of my hand. He folded like three hearts to the ten. I wrestled the storeroom door open, dragged him inside, and stepped over him to close the door. All quiet. I worked his black coat and trousers off, unhooked the stiff white dickey and tie. He snored softly. I pulled the clothes on over the weather-suit. They were a fair fit; he was tall and overweight. By the light of my pencil flash, I cut down a heavy braided cord hanging by a high window, used it to truss the waiter's hands and feet together behind him, tucked him in behind a crate, and stepped back out into the hall. Still quiet. I tried one of the drinks; it wasn't bad. I took another, ditched the empties, then picked up the tray and followed the sounds of music.

11

The grand ballroom was a hundred yards long, fifty wide, with walls of dusty rose, gold, and white. The banks of high windows were hung with crimson velvet; a vaulted ceiling was decorated with cherubs. On the polished acre of floor gaudily gowned and uniformed couples moved in stately time to the heavy beat of the traditional foxtrot. All the women, distributed strictly one to a man, were young and at least fairly good-looking. No wallflowers, no duennas. I moved slowly along the edge of the crowd, looking for someone who fit the description of the Baron—five-ten, thin black hair, sharp nose . . .

A hand caught my arm and hauled me around; a glass fell off my tray, smashed on the floor. A dapper little man in a black-and-white headwaiter's uniform glared up at me.

"What do you think you're doing, cretin?" he hissed.

"That's the genuine ancient stock you're slopping on the floor, boss," I told him. I looked around; no one else seemed to be paying any attention . . .

"Where are you from?" he snarled.

I opened my mouth for the snappy comeback—

"Never mind, you're all the same," he growled. He wagged his hands disgustedly. "The pack-rats they send me—a disgrace to the Black. Now, you! Stand up! Hold your tray proudly, gracefully! Step along daintily, not like a knight taking the field! And pause occasionally—just on the chance that some noble guest might wish to drink!"

"You bet, pal," I said. I moved on, paying a little more attention to my waiting. I saw plenty of green uniforms; pea green, forest green, emerald green—but they were all hung with braid and medals. According to Pop, the Baron affected a spartan simplicity—the diffidence of absolute power.

There were high white-and-gold doors every few yards along the side of the ballroom. I spotted one standing open and sidled toward it; it wouldn't hurt to reconnoiter the area. . . .

Just beyond the door, a very large sentry in a bottle green uniform with seven stripes moved to block me. He was dressed like a toy soldier, but there was nothing playful about the way he snapped his power gun to the ready. I winked at him.

"Thought you boys might want a drink," I hissed. "Rum—the good stuff; light as ether."

He looked at the tray, licked his lips, but didn't bite. "Get back in there, you fool," he growled. "You'll get us both hung . . ."

"Suit yourself, pal," I said agreeably and started to back out, slowly; just before the door closed between us, he lifted a glass off the tray. I eased back inside and almost collided with a long, lean cookie in a powder-blue outfit complete with dress saber, gold frogs, leopard-skin facings, a pair of

knee-length white gloves looped under an epau-
lette, a pistol in a fancy holster, and an eighteen-
inch swagger stick. He gave me the kind of look
old maids give sin.

"Look where you're going, swine," he said in a
voice like a pine board splitting.

"Have a drink, Admiral," I suggested.

He lifted his upper lip to show me a row of
teeth that hadn't had their annual trip to the dentist lately. The ridges along each side of his mouth
turned greenish white. He snatched for the gloves
on his shoulder, fumbled them; they slapped the
floor beside me.

"I'd pick those up for you, Chief," I said. "But
I've got my tray . . ."

He drew a breath between his teeth, chewed it
into strips, and snorted it back at me, then snapped
his fingers and pointed with his stick toward the
door behind me, the one I'd just come through.

"Come along; open that, instantly!" he snapped.
It didn't seem like the time to argue. I pulled the
door open and he stepped through with me right
beside him. The guard in green ducked his glass
and snapped to attention when he saw the baby-
blue outfit. My new friend ignored him, made a
curt gesture, calling me to heel. I trailed him
along the wide, high, gloomy corridor to a small
door, pushed through it into a well-lit, tile-walled
latrine with the Hilton logo in each tile. A big-
eyed slave in white ducks stared. Blue Boy jerked
his head at him. The slave scuttled away. Blue
Boy turned to me.

"Strip off your jacket, slave," he ordered. "Your
owner has neglected to teach you discipline."

I looked around quickly, saw that we were alone.

"Wait a minute while I put the tray down, Corporal," I said. "We don't want to waste any of the good stuff."

I turned to put the tray on a soiled-linen bin, caught a glimpse of motion in the mirror. I ducked and a nasty-looking little leather quirt whistled past my ear, slammed against the edge of a marble-topped lavatory with a crack like a pistol shot. I dropped the tray, stepped in fast, and threw a left at Blue Boy's jaw that bounced his head against the tiled wall; I followed up with a right to the belt-buckle, then held him up as he bent over, gagging, and hit him hard under the ear.

I hauled him into a booth, propped him up, and started shedding the waiter's blacks.

12

I left him snoring on the floor wearing my old suit, and stepped out into the hall, all in blue now. I liked the feel of his pistol at my hip. It was a well-worn issue .38, the same model I favored. The blue uniform was a good fit, what with the weight I'd lost. Blue Boy and I had something in common after all.

Out in the corridor, the exiled latrine attendant goggled at me. I grimaced like a quadruple amputee trying to scratch his nose and jerked my head toward the door I had come out of; I hoped the gesture would look familiar.

"Truss that mad dog and throw him outside the gates," I snarled. I stamped off down the corridor, trying to look mad enough to discourage curiosity. Apparently it worked; a few people passed, but nobody yelled for the cops.

I reentered the ballroom by another door, snagged a drink off a passing tray, checked over the crowd. I saw two more powder blue get-ups, Jersey big-shots, as I learned eventually, so I wasn't unique enough to draw special attention. I made a mental note to stay well away from my comrades in blue, and blended with the landscape, chatting and nodding and not neglecting my drinking, working my way toward a big arched doorway on the other side of the room that looked like the kind of entrance the head man might use. I didn't want to meet him—not yet. I just wanted to get him located before I went any further.

A passing wine slave poured a full inch of the genuine ancient stock into my glass, ducked his head, and moved on. I gulped it like sour bar whiskey; my attention was elsewhere. A flurry of activity near the big door indicated that maybe my guess had been accurate. Potbellied officials were forming up in a sort of reception line near the big double door. I started to drift back into the rear rank, bumped against a fat man in gray with medals and a sash, who glared, fingered a monocle with a plump ring-studded hand, and said, "Suggest you take your place, Colonel," in a suety voice.

I must have looked doubtful, because he bumped me with his paunch and growled, "Foot of the line next to the Earl's equerry, you idiot." He elbowed me aside and waddled past. I took a step after him, reached out with my left foot, and hooked his shiny black boot. He leaped forward, off-balance, medals jangling. I did a fast fade while he was still groping for his monocle, eased into a spot at the end of the line.

The conversation had died away to a nervous murmur. The doors swung back and a pair of guards with more trimmings than a phony stock certificate stamped into view, wheeled to face each other, and presented arms—chrome-plated automatic rifles, in this case. A dark-faced old man of medium height, with thin gray hair, a nose that had been socked pretty hard once, and a trimmed grey Vandyke came into view, limping slightly from a stiffish knee. His unornamented grey outfit made him as conspicuous in this gathering as a crane among peacocks. He nodded perfunctorily to the left and right, coming along between the waiting rows of flunkies who snapped to as he came abreast, then wilted and let out sighs behind him. I thought there was something familiar about him, but I couldn't place it. He looked about seventy, give or take the age of a bottle of second-rate bourbon, with the weather-beaten complexion of a former outdoorsman and the same look of alertness grown bored that a rattlesnake farmer develops—just before the fatal bite. He looked up and caught my eye on him, and for a moment I thought he hesitated as though he were about to speak. Then he went on past. At the end of the line, he turned abruptly and spoke to a man who nodded and hurried away. Then he engaged in conversation with a cluster of head-bobbing guests—but I knew damn well I'd been spotted.

I spent the next fifteen minutes casually getting close to the green door nearest the one the Baron had entered by. I looked around; nobody was paying any attention to me. The Baron's back was turned. I stepped past a guard who presented arms; the door closed softly, cutting off the buzz of talk and the worst of the music.

I went along to the end of the corridor. From the transverse hall, a grand staircase rose in a sweep of bright chrome and pale wood. I didn't know where it led, but it looked right. I headed for it, moving along briskly like a man with important business in mind and no time for light chitchat.

13

Two flights up, in a wide corridor of muted lights, ankle-deep carpets, brocaded wall hangings, mirrors, urns, and an odor of expensive tobacco and *Cuir de Russie*, a small man in black bustled from a side corridor, saw me, opened his mouth, closed it, half turned away, then swung back to face me. I recognized him; he was the headwaiter who had pointed out the flaws in my waiting style half an hour earlier.

"Here—" he started.

I chopped him short with a roar of what I hoped was authentic upper-crust rage.

"Direct me to his Excellency's apartments, scum!" I bellowed. "And thank your guardian imp I'm in too great haste to cane you for the insolent look about you!"

If he resented any of that, he didn't say so; instead, he went pale, gulped hard, and pointed. I snorted and stamped past him down the turning he had indicated.

This was Baronial country, all right. A pair of guards at the far end of the corridor looked my way. I'd passed half a dozen with no more than a click of their heels to indicate they saw me; these two shouldn't be any different—and it wouldn't look good if I turned and started back at the sight of them. The first rule of the gatecrasher is to act as if you belong where you are.

When I was fifty feet from them, they both shifted rifles—not to a present-arms position, but at the ready, nickel-plated bayonets aimed right at me. It was no time for me to look doubtful; I kept on coming. At twenty feet, I heard their rifle bolts snick home. I stopped ten feet from them. I could see the expressions on their faces now; they looked as nervous as a couple of teenaged sailors on their first visit to a joy-house.

"Point those butter knives into the corner, you banana-fingered cotton-choppers!" I said, looking bored and only slightly annoyed. The guns didn't waver. I unlimbered my swagger stick and slapped my gloved hand with it, letting them think it over. The gun muzzles dropped—just slightly. I followed up fast.

"Which is the anteroom to the Baron's apartment?" I demanded.

"Uh . . . this here is His Excellency's apartments, sir, but is the Colonel cleared for—"

"Never mind the lecture, you milk-faced fool," I cut in. "Do you think I'd be here if it weren't? Which is the anteroom, damn you!"

"We got orders, sir," he said in a hoarse whisper, as if he didn't want to hear what he was saying. "Nobody's to come closer than that last door back there—"

"We got orders to shoot!" the other interrupted. He was a little older, maybe twenty-two. I turned on him.

"I'm waiting for an answer to a question!" I said in a tone like a loaded freightcar squashing a beer can.

"Sir, the Articles—"

I narrowed my eyes. "I think you'll find paragraph Two-B covers Special Cosmic Top Secret couriers," I told him. "When you two recruits go off duty, report yourselves on punishment. Now, the anteroom! And be quick about it!"

The bayonets were sagging now. The younger of the two licked his lips. "Sir, we never been inside. We don't know how it's laid out in there. If the Colonel wants to just take a look . . ."

The other guard opened his mouth to say something. I didn't wait to find out what it was. I stepped between them, muttering something about bloody recruits and important messages, and worked the fancy handle on the big gold and white door. I paused to give the two sentries a hard look.

"I hope I don't have to remind you that any mention of the movements of a Cosmic courier is punishable by slow death. Just forget you ever saw me." I went on in and closed the door without waiting to catch the reaction to that one.

14

The Baron had done well by himself in the matter of decor. The room I was in—a sort of lounge-cum-bar—was paved in two-inch-deep nylon fuzz the color of a fog at sea. The carpet foamed up at the edges against walls of pale blue brocade with tiny yellow flowers. The bar was a teak log split down the middle and polished, and the glasses sitting on it were like tissue-paper engraved with patterns of nymphs and satyrs. Subdued light came from somewhere, along with a faint melody that seemed to speak of youth and love, long ago.

I went on into the next room, found more soft light, the glow of hand-rubbed rare woods, rich fabrics, and wide windows with a view of dark night sky. The music was coming from a long, low, built-in speaker topped with a lamp, a heavy crystal ashtray, and a display of hothouse roses. There was a scent in the air—not the *Cuir de Russie* and Havana leaf I'd smelled in the hall, but a subtler perfume. . . .

I turned—and looked into the eyes of a girl with long black lashes, glossy black hair that came down to bare shoulders. An arm as smooth and white as whipped cream was draped over a chair back, the hand holding a six-inch cigarette holder and sporting a diamond as inconspicuous as a chrome-plated hubcap.

"You must want something pretty badly," she murmured, batting her eyelashes at me. I could feel the breeze at ten feet. I nodded. Under the circumstances, that was about the best I could do.

"What could it be," she mused, "that's worth being impaled for?" Her voice was like the rest of her: smooth, polished, and relaxed—and with plenty of moxie held in reserve. She smiled casually, drew on her cigarette, tapped ashes onto the priceless rug.

"Something bothering you, Colonel?" she inquired. "You don't seem talkative."

"I'll do my talking when the Baron arrives," I said.

"In that case, Jackson," said a reedy voice behind me, "you can start any time you like . . ."

I held my hands clear of my body and turned around slowly—just in case there was a nervous gun aimed at my spine. The Baron was standing near the door, unarmed, relaxed. There were no guards in sight. The girl looked mildly amused. I put my hand on my pistol butt.

"How do you know my name?" I asked.

The Baron waved toward a chair. "Sit down, Jackson," he said, almost gently. "You've had a tough time of it—but you're all right now." He walked past me to the bar, poured out two glasses, turned and offered me one. I felt a little silly standing there fingering the gun. I went over and took the drink.

"To the old days." The Baron raised his glass.

I drank; it was the genuine ancient stock, all right; it made the rum seem like Exxon Regular.

"I asked you how you know my name," I said.

"That's easy; I used to know you. . . ." He smiled faintly. There was still something about his face . . .

"You look well in the uniform of the Penn Dragoons," he said. "Better than you ever did in Aerospace blue."

"Good God," I said. "Tobey Mallon . . ."

He ran a hand over his nearly-bald head. "A little less hair on top, plus a beard as compensation, a few wrinkles, a slight pot. Oh, I've changed, Jackson."

"I had it figured as close to eighty years," I said. "The trees, the condition of the buildings—"

"Not far off the mark; seventy-eight years this spring."

"You're a well-preserved hundred and ten, Tobey."

He shook his head. "You weren't the only one in the tanks—but you had a better unit than I did. Mine gave out twenty years ago."

"You mean—you walked into this cold—just like I did?"

He nodded. "I know how you feel. Rip Van Winkle had nothing on us."

"Just one question, Tobey. The men you sent to pick me up seemed more interested in shooting than talking. I almost didn't get here. I'm wondering why."

Mallon threw out his hand. "A little misunderstanding, Jackson. I've had the fool executed. You made it; that's all that counts. Now that you're here, we've got some planning to do together. I haven't had it easy these last twenty years. I started off with nothing: first I organized some locals, a few hundred scavengers living in the ruins, hiding out every time Jersey or Dee-Cee raided for supplies. I built an organization, started a systematic salvage operation. I saved everything I could find that the rats and weather hadn't gotten to, spruced up my palace here and stocked it. It's a rich province, Jackson—"

"And now you own it all." It didn't sound as sarcastic as I intended. "Not bad, Tobey."

He preened a little. "They say knowledge is power; I had the necessary knowledge." He sounded satisfied.

I finished my drink and put the glass on the bar.

"What's this planning you say we have to do?"

Mallon leaned back on one elbow. "Jackson, it's been a long haul—alone. It's good to see an old shipmate. But before we talk details, we'll dine. If you feel the way I did, you can use it."

I must have looked doubtful, because he added, "No cans, of course. No," he went on complacently. "I have a few pigs and chickens in the Patio Garden, and a kitchen garden in the Pool Garden. I grew up on a farm, you know, before I got interested in physics."

"I might manage to nibble a little something— say a horse, roasted whole," I told him, meaning it. "Don't bother to remove the saddle. I'll spit out the shoes."

He laughed, wheezily. "First we eat," he said. "Then we conquer the world."

15

I squeezed the last drop from the Beaujolais bottle, and watched the girl, whose name was Renada, hold a light for the cigar Mallon had taken from a silver box. My blue mess jacket and holster hung over the back of the chair. Everything was cosy now.

"Time for business, Jackson," Mallon said. He blew out smoke and looked at me through it. "How did things look—inside?"

"Dusty, but intact, below ground level. Upstairs, there's blast damage and weathering. I don't suppose it's changed much since you came out twenty years ago. As far as I could tell, the Primary Site is okay. I saw some signs of tampering."

Mallon nodded and leaned forward. "Now, you made it out past the Bolo. How did it handle itself? Still fully functional?"

I sipped my wine, thinking over my answer, remembering the Bolo's empty guns . . .

"It damn near gunned me down," I said, sounding disgusted. "It's getting a little old and it can't see as well as it used to, but it's still a tough baby."

Mallon swore suddenly. "It was Mackenzie's idea; a last-minute move when the evacuation order came through. It was a pinpoint bombardment—by our own Air Force, you know."

71

"I hadn't heard. How did you find out all this?"

Mallon shot me a sharp look. "There were still a few people around who'd been in it; then there were the old newspapers—but never mind that. What about *Prometheus*? She's still unlooted, of course? That's what we're interested in. Fuel, weapons, even some nuclear stuff. The food supplies, and the prime movers. Maybe we'll even find one or two of the Colossus missiles still in their silos. I made an air recon a few years back, before my chopper broke down—"

"I think two silo doors are still in place; but why the interest in armament?"

Mallon snorted. "You've got a few things to learn about the setup, Jackson," he sneered. "I need that stuff. If I hadn't lucked into a stock of weapons and ammo in the Admin vault, Jersey would be wearing the spurs in my palace right now!"

I drew on my cigar and let the silence stretch out. "You said something about conquering the world, Tobey. I don't suppose by any chance you meant that literally?"

Mallon stood up, his closed fists working like a man crumpling unpaid bills. "They all want what I've got, what I made here! They're all waiting for a sign of weakness." He walked across the room, back. "I'm ready to move against them now! I can put four thousand trained men in the field—"

"Let's get a couple of things straight, Mallon," I cut in. "You've got the natives fooled with this Baron routine—but don't try it on me. Maybe it was even necessary once; maybe there's an excuse for some of the stories I've heard. That's over now. I'm not interested in tribal warfare or gang rumbles. I need—"

"Better remember who's running things here, Jackson," Mallon snapped. "It's not what *you* need that counts." He took another turn up and down the room, then stopped, facing me. "Look, Jackson; I know how to get around in this jungle; you don't. If I hadn't spotted you and given some orders, you'd have been gunned down before you left the garage. Your men ran out on you, you know."

"Why'd you let me in?" I was genuinely curious. "I might've been gunning for you."

"You clearly wanted to see the Baron alone; that suited me, too. If word got out—" He broke off, cleared his throat. "Let's stop wrangling, Jackson. We can't move until the Bolo guarding the site has been neutralized. There's only one way to do that: knock it out! And the only thing that can knock out a Bolo is another Bolo."

"So?"

"I've *got* another Bolo, Jackson. It's been covered, maintained. It can go against the Troll—" He broke off, laughed shortly. "That's what the mob calls it."

"You could have done that years ago; where do I come in?"

"You're checked out on a Mark III, Jackson. You know something about this kind of equipment."

"Sure. So do you."

"I never learned," he said shortly.

"Who's kidding who, Mallon? We all took the same orientation course less than a month ago—"

"For me it's been a long month; let's just say I've forgotten."

"You parked that Bolo at your front gate and then forgot how you did it, eh?"

"Nonsense; it's always been there."

I shook my head. "I know different."

Mallon looked wary. "Where'd you get that idea?"

"Somebody told me."

Mallon ground his cigar out savagely on the damask cloth. "You'll point the scum out to me—"

"Don't blow a gasket, Mallon. What makes it important?"

"Whoever it was, he was lying! I never moved the Bolo."

"Then why was it here, miles from the site?"

"How do I know?" he snarled defensively. "There was chaos here, Jackson; riots, mob rule. Maybe it was somebody's idea of a defensive move, but something went wrong."

"I don't give a damn whether you moved it or not. Anybody with your training can figure out the controls of a Bolo in half an hour—"

"Not well enough to take on the Tr— another Bolo."

I took a cigar from the silver box, picked up the lighter from the table, turned the cigar in the flame. Suddenly, it was very quiet in the room. I looked across at Mallon. He held out his hand. His eyes were on the lighter.

"I'll take that," he said shortly.

I blew out smoke, squinted through it at Mallon. He sat with his hand out, waiting. I looked down at the lighter. It was a heavy windproof model, with embossed Aerospace wings. I turned it over; engraved letters read: LIEUTENANT COMMANDER DON G. BANNER, USN. I looked up. Renada sat quietly, holding my pistol trained dead on my belt buckle.

16

"I'm sorry you saw that," Mallon said. "It could cause misunderstandings . . ."

"Where's Banner?"

"He . . . died. I told you—"

"You told me a lot of things, Tobey. Some of them might even be true. Did you make him the same offer you've made me?"

Mallon darted a look at Renada; she sat, holding the pistol, looking at me distantly, without expression.

"You've got the wrong idea, Jackson—" Mallon started.

"You and he came out about the same time, I guess," I said. "Or maybe you got the jump on him by a few days. It must have been close; otherwise you'd never have taken him. Don was a sharp boy."

"You're out of your mind!" Mallon snapped. "Why, I cycled him out! Don Banner was my friend—"

"Then why do you get nervous when I find his lighter on your table? There could be ten perfectly harmless explanations—"

"I don't make explanations," Mallon said flatly.

"That attitude is hardly the basis for a lasting

partnership, Tobey. I have an unhappy feeling there's something you're not telling me."

Mallon pulled himself up in the chair. "Look here, Jackson, we've no reason to fall out. There's plenty for both of us. And one day I'll be needing a successor; don't forget—Don was a direct competitor, but I've aged twenty years more than you. It was too bad about Banner, but that's ancient history now. Forget it. What's important is that we end this foolish dispute. I want you with me, Jackson! Together we can rule the Atlantic seaboard —or even more!"

I drew on my cigar, looking at the gun in Renada's hand. "You hold all the aces, Tobey. Shooting me would be no trick at all— "

"There's no trick involved, Jackson!" Mallon snapped. "After all," he went on, almost wheedling now, "we're old friends. I want to give you a break, share with you—"

"I don't think I'd trust him if I were you, Mr. Jackson," Renada's quiet voice cut in. I looked at her. She looked back calmly. "You're more important to him than you think," she added quietly.

"Renada," Mallon barked. "Go to your room at once."

"Not just yet, Tobey," she said. "I'm also curious about how my ancestor died." The gun in her hand wasn't pointed at me now; it was aimed at Mallon's chest.

17

Mallon sat, sunk deep in his chair, looking at me with eyes like a python with a bellyache. "You're fools, both of you," he grated. "I gave you everything, Renada; I've raised you like my own daughter. And you, Jackson. You could have shared with me— all of it."

"I don't need a share of your delusions, Tobey," I said. "I've got a full set of my own. But before we go any further, let's clear up a few points. Why haven't you been getting any mileage out of your pet Bolo? And what makes *me* important in the picture?"

"He's afraid," Renada said. "There's a spell on it which prevents men from approaching—even the Baron."

"Shut your mouth, you fool!" Mallon choked on his fury. I tossed the lighter in my hand and felt a smile twitching at my mouth.

"So Don was too smart for you after all. He must have been the one who had control of the Bolo. I suppose you called for a truce, and then shot him from under the white flag. But he fooled you; he plugged a command into the Bolo's circuits to fire on anyone who came close—unless he was Banner."

"You're crazy!" Mallon snarled, with plenty of spit.

"It's close enough," I told him. "You can't get near the Bolo, right? And after twenty years, the bluff you've been running on the other barons with your pet troll must be getting a little thin. Any day now, one of them may decide to try you . . ."

Mallon twisted his face in what may have been an attempt at a placating smile. "I won't argue with you, Jackson. You're right about the command circuit; Banner set it up to fire an anti-personnel blast at anyone coming within fifty yards. He did it to keep the mob from tampering with the machine. But there's a loophole. It wasn't only Banner who could get close; he set it up to accept any of the *Prometheus* crew—except me. He hated me; it was a trick, to try to get me killed."

"So you're figuring I'll step in and defuse her for you, eh, Tobey? Well, I'm sorry as hell to disappoint you, but somehow in the confusion I left my electropass behind."

Mallon leaned toward me. "I told you we need each other, Jackson! I've got your pass; yours and all the others. Renada, hand me my black box." She rose, moved across to the desk, still holding the gun aimed at him.

"Where'd you get my pass, Mallon?" I asked.

"Where do you think? They're the duplicates that were in the vault in the old command block. I knew one day one of you would come out. I'll tell you, Jackson, it's been hell, waiting all these years—and hoping. I gave orders that any time the Lesser Troll bellowed, the mob was to form up to help my troops stop anybody who came out. I don't know how you got through them . . ."

"I was too slippery for them. Besides," I added, "I met a friend."

"A friend? Who's that?"

"An old man who thought I was Prince Charming, come to wake everybody up. He was nuts, but he got me through."

Renada came back, handed me a square steel box. "Give him the key, Tobey," she ordered quietly. He handed it over. I opened the box, sorted through half a dozen silver dollar-sized ovals of clear plastic, lifted out the one with my ID on it.

"Is it a magical charm?" Renada asked, sounding awed. She didn't seem so sophisticated now—but I liked her better human.

"Just a synthetic crystalline plastic, designed to resonate to a pattern peculiar to my EEG," I said. "It amplifies the signal and gives off a characteristic emission that the psychotronic circuit in the Bolo picks up—"

"That's what I thought," she said, nodding. "Magic."

"Call it magic, then, kid." I dropped the pass in my pocket, stood and looked at Renada. "I don't doubt that you know how to use that gun, Honey—but I'm leaving now. Try not to shoot me."

"You're a fool if you try it," Mallon barked. "If Renada doesn't shoot you, my guards will—and even if you made it, you'd still need me!"

"I'm touched by your concern, Tobey," I told him. "All right, you've got two minutes to convince me. Start talking!"

"You wouldn't get past the first sentry post without my help, Jackson," Mallon ranted. "These people know me as the Trollmaster. They're in awe of me—of my *mana*. But together, we can get to the controls of the Bolo, then use it to knock out the sentry machine at the Site—"

"Then what?" I wanted to know. "With an operating Bolo I don't need you," I reminded him. "Better improve the picture, Tobey. I'm not impressed."

He wet his lips. "It's *Prometheus*, don't you understand? She's stocked with everything from Browning needlers to Norge stunners. Tools, weapons, instruments—and the main ion drive, Jackson—"

"I don't need toys if I own a Bolo, Tobey. And the ion drive is useless except to do what it was built for."

Mallon sneered. "Don't tell *me* what the ion drive can do, Whiz. *I'm* the expert, remember? I was the one who came up with the idea of the energy sink in the first place. What I don't know about it isn't worth knowing."

"They call it megalomania," I told him.

Mallon used some profanity. "You'll leave your liver and lights on the palace altar, Jackson, I promise you that—"

"Tell him what he wants to know, Tobey," Renada said.

Mallon narrowed his eyes on her. "You'll live to regret this, Renada . . ."

"Maybe I will, Tobey. But you taught me how to handle a gun—and to play cards for keeps."

The flush faded out of his face and left it pale. "All right, Jackson," he said, almost in a whisper. "It's not only the equipment; it's . . . the men."

I heard a clock humming somewhere.

"What men, Tobey?" I said softly.

"The crew. Day, Macy, the others. They're still in there, Jackson—aboard the ship, in stasis. We

were still trying to get the ship off when the
Collapse came. There was plenty of warning that
the mob was coming, howling for blood. Everything was ready to go. You and Banner were already in; there wasn't time to cycle the primary
crew . . . I went in hoping—but no one could be
sure I'd ever come out. . . ."

"Keep talking."

"You know how the system was set up; it was to
be a nine-year run out, with an automatic turn-
around at the end of that time if Jupiter wasn't
within design range." He snorted. "It wasn't, of
course. After a twenty-year cruise, still in her
dock, her instruments checked again. She was pro-
tected against everything but what happened: an
abort at launch minus three seconds. Some timing:
the automatics didn't know about that. They ran
checks and detected one G of gravity and thirty
percent-plus O_2 ambient—all well within design
parameters—so they were satisfied: there was a
planetary mass within the acceptable range. So
after the third check they brought me out." He
snorted again. "The longest dry run in history. I
unstrapped, and came out to see what was going
on. It took me a little while to realize what had
happened. I went back and cycled Banner and
Johnny out. We went into the town; you know
what we found. I saw what we had to do, but
Banner and Black argued. The fools wanted to
reseal *Prometheus* and proceed with the launch.
For what? So we could spend the rest of our lives
squatting in the ruins, when by stripping the ship
we could make ourselves kings?"

"There's more, Mr. Jackson," Renada said steadily. "Tell it all, Tobey."

He turned to glare at her. "Can't you keep your damned mouth shut, you ungrateful slut?" he snarled, and then turned back to me. "Very well: it's the ion-drive, of course. You know it was so designed—and I was on the design team—as to be converted to ground power once we were safely down on Callisto. At full bore the coil produces as a by-product over a million megawatts of direct electric current. One of the big problems in the project was disposing of it harmlessly, you'll recall."

I nodded. "Sure, the energy sink was what all the subsurface installation was for. What about it?"

"Surely you can see, once it's pointed out to you," he said contemptuously. "What does this tower, this whole province need, Jackson? Energy, that's what! All the generator plants are off-line, but the distribution system is still intact. All that's required is a power source, and all these dead channels will work again! Lights will go on, washing machines and TV sets and air conditioners will come to life! Talk about *mana*! Once I've done that for the populace, there'll be no more malcontents!"

"Just how do you propose to shunt this million megawatts into the tea cozies and wall-clocks without blowing *Prometheus* and everything else into a thin gas?" I wanted to know. "On Callisto, the coil would have been reinstalled outside the hull."

He was grinning from ear to ear and nodding. "That's where my genius comes into play," he told me. "And my training: I was power officer, remember? Dammit, man, I've already done it! I collected every scrap of copper and silver in the city—in the whole province! We poured buss bars in place, and I rigged the sink to act as a transformer and stepped it down. Tied the main line into the county system. All that's needed now is to fire her up! Then, of course, I have the final connection-to-line switch rigged here. Right in this room!" He pointed to a big circuit-breaker mounted on a crude console.

"I see," I told him. "I take it all that was before the Troll went on duty."

Tobey snarled. "That was Mackenzie's fault, the fool! At the last he turned against me, said the men aboard would die if anything went wrong. Think of it!" Tobey threw out his hands. "To throw away an empire on the chance that a few men *might* die. Now, *that's* madness!"

"So there was an argument?" I prompted.

"I had a gun. I didn't want to use it, but they forced my hand. I hit Johnny in the leg, I think—but they got clear, found a car, and beat me to the Site. There were two Bolos in the bunker. What chance did I have against them?"

Mallon grinned craftily. "But Banner was a fool. He died for it." The grin dropped like a stripper's bra. "But when I went to claim my spoils, I discovered how the jackals had set the trap for me."

"That was downright unfriendly of them, Mallon. Oddly enough, it doesn't make me want to stay and hold your hand."

"Don't you understand *yet?*" Mallon's voice was a dry screech. "Even if you got clear of the Palace, and used the Bolo to set yourself up as Baron, you'd never be safe—not as long as one man was still alive aboard the ship. You'd never have a night's rest, wondering when one of them would walk out to challenge your rule . . ."

"Uneasy lies the head, eh, Tobey? You remind

me of a queen bee: the first one out of the chrysalis stings all her rivals to death."

The waiter arrived then, accompanied by aromas that made my jaws ache. We ate chicken Kiev from Haviland china, and sipped a fine vintage from paper-thin Orefors glass.

"What do Day and his crew get out of your scheme, Tobey?" I asked him over the coffee.

"I don't mean to kill them, of course," he growled. "That would be a waste of trained men. I mean to give them useful work to do."

"I don't think they'd like being your slaves, Tobey," I said. "And neither would I." I looked at Renada. "I'll be leaving you now," I said. "Whichever way you decide, good luck."

"Wait," she stood, and moved around behind my chair. "I'm going with you," she said without emphasis.

I looked over at her. "I'll be travelling fast, honey—and that gun in my back may throw off my timing." Keeping my eye on Tobey, I stood.

She stepped to me, reversed the pistol and laid it in my hand. "Don't kill him, Mr. Jackson. He was always kind to me," she said.

"Are you sure?" I asked her. "According to good old Uncle Tobey, my chances don't look good."

"I never knew before how Commander Banner died," she said. "He was my great-grandfather."

I remembered how proud Don had been of his baby girl—Renada's grandmother.

Renada came back bundled in a gray fur as I finished buckling on my holster.

"So long, Tobey," I said. "I ought to shoot you in the belly just for Don—but—"

I saw Renada's eyes widen at the same instant

that I heard the click. She stepped aside. I dropped flat and rolled behind Mallon's chair—and a gout of blue flame yammered into the spot where I'd been standing. I whipped the gun up and put a round into the peach-colored upholestery an inch from Tobey's ear. His head jerked a little; his nerves were OK. They didn't pick wimps to crew *Prometheus*.

"The next one nails you to the chair," I yelled. "Call 'em off!" There was a moment of dead silence. Tobey sat frozen. I couldn't see who'd been doing the shooting. Then I heard a moan behind me: Renada . . .

"Let the girl alone or I'll kill him," I called.

Tobey sat rigid, his eyes rolled toward me.

"You can't kill me, Jackson," he whined. "I'm all that's keeping you alive . . ."

"You can't kill me either, Tobey," I yelled back. "You need my magic touch, remember? Maybe you'd better give us a safe-conduct out of here; I'll take the freeze off your Bolo—if you cooperate."

Tobey licked his lips. I heard Renada again. She was trying not to moan—but moaning anyway. "Don't do it, Jacks—" she blurted.

"You tried, Jackson; it didn't work out," Tobey said through gritted teeth. "Throw down that weapon and walk over there." He nodded to indicate where "there" was. "I won't let them kill you—you know that much," he grated. "You do as you're told and you may still live to a ripe old age—and the girl, too."

She screamed then—a mindless ululation of pure agony.

"Hurry up, you fool, before they tear her arm off," Mallon snarled. "Or shoot. You'll get to watch her for twenty-four hours under the knife; then you'll have your turn."

I fired again—closer. Mallon jerked his head a little harder this time. He cursed.

"If they touch her again, you get it, Tobey," I said. "Send her over here. Move!"

"Let her go!" Mallon snarled. Renada stumbled into sight, from behind me, cradling her left arm; then she crumpled suddenly to the rug beside me.

"Stand up, Tobey," I ordered. He got to his feet slowly. Sweat was glistening on his face now. "Stand over here," I ordered. He moved like a sleep-walker. I risked a quick glance over my shoulder. There were two men standing across the room beside a small open door—a sliding panel. Both of them held power rifles leveled, but aimed off-side, well away from the Baron—and me.

"Drop 'em!" I said. They didn't move until Mallon made a grunting sound. They looked at me, then lowered the guns, tossed the weapons aside; they seemed to take a long time to fall. I opened my mouth to tell Mallon to move over to the wall, but my tongue felt thick and heavy. Suddenly the room was full of smoke. In front of me, Mallon was wavering like a mirage. I started to tell him to stand still, but with my thick tongue, it was too much trouble. That fine vintage had been doped.

I raised the gun, but somehow it was falling to the floor, slowly, like a leaf—and then I was floating, too, on waves that broke on a dark sea . . .

18

Renada was standing over me when I came to. It took me a while to realize I was lying on that fat rug. My brain was getting woozy from being hit over the head, and now I'd been doped, too. I didn't see Tobey. Renada had the gun again and from the look of the two corpses over by the door, she indeed knew how to use it. She smiled down at me. "Get up, Jackson," she suggested. "I get tired of holding this thing."

"Where's Tobey?" I wanted to know. I got up, all right, but it wasn't easy. I was still half-dopey.

"He ran for it," she said, almost but not quite sneering. Those perfect lips could never sneer. "I let him go."

"That was wise of you, my dear," Mallon's voice spoke up. "I'll remember it at your trial." I looked past Renada, saw him ease into the room via the sliding panel in the corner, holding his issue .38 aimed squarely at the girl's back.

"Drop it, honey," I told her. "And you can call me 'Jack.'" She let the weapon fall and turned to face Mallon.

While his attention was all on her, I scooped up my old .38, and checked the cylinder: it still held four. I snapped it shut and aimed at the center of Tobey's forehead, trying not to waver. He heard the *click!* and his eyes cut from Renada to me. He held the grin for a moment and then it collapsed into a snarl, but he didn't fire.

"You wouldn't dare, Whiz," he grated—but took a step backward. "You know your treachery isn't going to do you any good." He sounded almost contented. "You walked right into the killing chamber of a very large and secure trap." He closed his hand as if it were closing on my neck.

"Freeze, Tobey!" I was fighting to keep my speech unslurred. "Or I might just do it," I improvised, "and work on the explanation later, after we've made a neat getaway through your trick panel."

He might not have altogether believed me, but he believed me enough to stay put. I told him to go into the closet and close the door. He started to bluster, but then he quickly masked a sly look and followed orders. The door closed on a look of fury like Satan being evicted from Heaven. I looked at Renada. She was sitting in one of the big fancy chairs, crying quietly.

"Why weren't you at the Grand Ball, having fun?" I asked her.

She shuddered. "I don't want you to think I'm Tobey's doxy."

"You mean you're *not*?"

She shuddered again. "I was fond of Tobey, of course," she said, "after all he did for me—but that was all. I thought of him as a sort of elder brother, I suppose, if that's the right term."

"Like an uncle, maybe," I suggested.

"You speak many strange words, Jack. Who are you, really?"

I didn't hear the question. "You're sure you want to throw all this over?" I insisted. "He might take you back, after a spanking."

"Now that I know the terrible things he did," she said, "I hate him."

"He wasn't a very nice fellow," I agreed. I went over and put an arm around her shoulder. "What now?"

She gave me a startled look, then nodded and took a moment to compose her face. "Yes," she said. "I suppose it *is* up to me to talk to Tobey and arrange a truce."

"Not quite. Where does the sliding panel lead?"

"I'm wondering," she replied dully, "why I should tell you." Her eyes went to the closet door.

"Uh-huh. You've got it made here. Why throw in with a loser who won't get ten steps down the secret passage?"

She turned with a sulky look and her eyes met mine. She stood. "Beats me, Jackson—Jack," she said. "What's your first name—really?"

"I never use it," I told her. "It's my grandmother's last name: 'Torrance.'"

"'Rance.'" She tried the name out. "I don't know," she went on. "I really don't know—except that you're a shipmate of Don Banner." She blinked back tears. "I hear he was a fine man," she added, and sniffled. My guess was that she'd been raised on stories of her revered ancestor until he loomed far, far larger than life. I went over and hugged her. "Good therapy, I understand—for both of us."

"All that talk of Tobey's about his *mana*," Renada said thoughtfully, "about removing the spell and restoring the old magic—does it mean anything at all? Is there really a way?"

"Tobey said so," I replied, wondering too, "and where ionics is involved, he's number one. He may have done it. At least he thinks he's done it."

"But—how?" she insisted. "Something about that *Prometheus*," she added vaguely.

"He meant to activate her main drive with the launch locks in place," I sort of explained. "Her ionic energy passing into the energy sink—*his* design, by the way—could be converted to electrical energy—or rather, the electrical components could be tapped off."

Renada was nodding, not so much in understanding as in encouragement.

"That was all a long time ago, kid," I reminded her. "This is now and we still have a couple of lives to live."

"That's a private lift," she told me, nodding toward the sliding door. "We can get directly to the garages."

I followed her to where Tobey had appeared. No sliding panel was visible. She touched a spot and the panel slid back. She started in and I blocked her, but she pushed past and turned to give me a defiant look.

"You'd better think this over, girl," I said. "Here, you've got it made. Out there, it's not so nice. And once I'm gone, Tobey will be eager to overlook any little indiscretion on your part."

She shook her head and her sleek hair swung. "He liked to give the impression I was his doxy," she said. "Actually he never touched me. He picked me up when I was nine years old, literally out of a garbage can. I was hiding from the soldiers," she added. "He raised me as a daughter." She paused to sob. "He had his good side."

"He did an amazing job," I told her. "You have all the little feminine ways—like the way you're blinking those teary eyelashes at me right now. I wouldn't have thought he could have done it. And that little stray curl behind your ear: it breaks my heart. Is that entirely accidental?"

She shook her head again in that instinctive way women have of the little gesture that makes a man turn to jelly.

"There was Woman," she corrected. "She was his real mistress, a long time ago. She was a wonderful lady; she taught me how to behave, and groom myself, and all the things only a woman would know. She helped protect me from his amorous ideas. In the end he exiled her, sent her off with only what she could carry. I hope she's all right."

"He watched his boys twist your arm," I commented. "But that's no big thing, really. You'd better stay put, kid. After a while you can let Tobey out and explain how you just lost your head for a minute."

"When I realized he'd actually killed Don Banner," she said dully, "that changed everything. I knew how cruel and ruthless he could be, but never to *me*. Killing Commander Banner changed that—completely. Come on, Rance, no time to waste."

"It's not just the fat life you're risking, girl," I

reminded her. "It's life itself. This place is swarming with Tobey's cops." I squeezed my eyes shut and shook my head to clear it. I was losing the thread of the conversation.

"They don't know I've turned against him," she pointed out. "And the Commander of the Guard, and quite a few other powerful men, are pals of mine. I've saved their necks more than once when Tobey threw a fit and was ready to order mass executions, and I stepped in and begged for them." This time she stepped into the six-by-six lift and turned to face me. "None of them would dare to interfere with me," she said with finality. "Even if they wanted to."

"Maybe," I said. "But why take the chance?"

"I don't change sides twice in one day," she told me coolly. "If I let you go down there alone, you'd never clear the first security point."

"You don't know what it's like out there," I said, feeling outvoted.

"I grew up for nine years out there," she reminded me. "I remember quite a lot. My folks, Bud and Marian,"—another sob—"might still be alive."

"Don't count on it. Things have gone downhill in the last few years, since the good water supply system failed." I wondered where I'd heard that.

"Then perhaps we can help," she said in a small voice.

I thought that was a bad time to try her again, "Look," I said, meaning it this time, "I'll go out and reconnoiter, and if it looks possible, I'll come back in a few days, and then we'll see."

She nodded. "I can give you the security codes,"

she said. "And a note for General Craig and the others, telling them Tobey and I have quarrelled, and you're on a mission for me." She stepped purposefully out of the lift, and stopped. She turned a stricken look on me.

"I forgot," she said suddenly, and turned toward the closet we'd locked Tobey in. "He has a signaler," she told me in a low voice. "I was a fool to forget. He always has it with him. We'll have to . . . kill him," she finished. "Before—"

But just then there were sounds at the door, then a gunshot and the latch blew out. Someone kicked the door and it *bang!*ed wide open and Tobey came through, flanked by two of his gunhandlers.

19

"Do you think you're the first idiot who thought he could kill me?" Mallon raised a contemptuous lip. "This room's rigged ten different ways." He gave Renada a venomous look, but she was watching me.

I shook my head, trying to ignore the remaining haze before my eyes and the nausea in my body. "No, I imagine lots of people would like a crack at you, Tobey," I conceded. "One day one of them's going to make it."

"Get him over here," Mallon snapped. A hand lifted my revolver; other hard hands clamped on my arms, manhandling me across the room: I worked my legs, exaggerating a little. I sagged against somebody who smelled like uncured hides.

"You seem drowsy," Mallon said, peering into my face. "We'll see if we can't wake you up."

A thumb dug into my neck; I jerked away, and a jab under the ribs doubled me over.

"I have to keep you alive—for the moment," Mallon said. "But you won't get a lot of pleasure out of it." I blinked hard; it was almost dark in the room now, except for a green-shaded lamp on the desk beside Tobey. One of my handlers had a ring of beard around his mouth—I could see that much. Renada wasn't in sight. Mallon came over to pose in front of me, his hands on his hips, grinning. I aimed a kick at him, just for fun. It didn't work out; my foot seemed to be wearing a lead boot. The unshaven man hit me in the mouth with the back of his hand; but I felt it all too distinctly: in the pain department, at least, I was almost clear of the dope-effects.

"Have some fun, Dunger," Tobey told his boy. "But I'll want him alive and on his feet for the night's work. Take him out and walk him in the fresh air. Report to me at the Pavillion of the Troll in an hour." He turned to someone I couldn't quite see and gave orders about lights and gun emplacements. I heard Renada's name mentioned. Then he was gone, and I was being dragged through the door and along the corridors.

It was chilly outside, with lots of lights glaring in the dark. The exercise helped. By the time the hour had passed, I was feeling weak but normal, except for an aching head and a feeling there was a strand of spiderweb interfering with my vision. Tobey had given me a good meal before the knuckles; maybe before the night was over, he'd regret that mistake.

They dropped me after a while, like a mouse the cat's tired of playing with. I lay where they left me and waited . . . for whatever was next.

Across the dark grounds an engine started up, sputtered, then settled down to a steady hum. The boys came back, hauled me upright. "It's time," the one with the whiskers said. He had a voice like soft cheese to match his smell. He took another half-twist in the arm he was holding.

"Don't break it," I grunted. "It belongs to the Baron, remember?"

Whiskers stopped dead. "You talk too much—and too smart." He let go and stepped back. "Hold him, Pig-Eye." The other man whipped a forearm across my throat and levered my head back; then Whiskers unlimbered the two-foot club from his belt and hit me hard in the side, just under the ribs. Pig-Eye let go and I folded over and waited while the pain swelled up and burst inside me. Then they hauled me back to my feet. I couldn't feel any broken ribs—if that was any consolation.

There were more lights glaring now from across the lawn; moving figures cast long shadows against the green-glowing trees lining the drive—and on the side of the Mark III Bolo Combat Unit parked under a sagging tarpaulin by the sealed gate. Crude breastworks had been thrown up about fifty yards from it. An old wheel-mounted generator *putt*ed noisily in the background, laying a light layer of bluish exhaust in the air. It was an old one-lung Commins diesel, built to last.

Mallon came up with what I had learned was a 9mm power rifle in his hands. My two guards gripped me with both hands to demonstrate their zeal; I was staggering a little more than was necessary. I saw Renada standing by, wrapped in her gray fur. Her face looked white in the harsh light. She made a move toward me and a greenback caught her arm—the same one they'd twisted before. She uttered one sharp cry and fainted. He caught her clumsily and held her upright.

"You know what to do, Jackson," Mallon said, speaking loudly against the clatter of the generator. He made a curt gesture and a man stepped up and buckled a stout chain to my left ankle. There was an insulated cable attached to it. Mallon held out my electropass. "I want you to walk straight to the Bolo," he told me in a bored voice. "Go in by the quarter port. You've got one minute to cancel the instructions punched into the command circuit and climb back outside. If you don't show in two minutes, I close a switch there"—he pointed to a wooden box mounting an open circuit breaker, with a tangle of heavy cable—"and you cook in your shoes. The same thing happens if I see the guns start to traverse, or the anti-personnel ports open."

I followed the coils of armored wire from the chain on my ankle to the wooden box—and on to the generator.

"Crude, maybe," Tobey commented, "but it will work. And if you get any idea of letting fly a round or two at random—remember the girl will be right beside me."

I looked across at the giant machine. "Suppose it doesn't recognize me?" I improvised. "It's been a while. Or what if Don *didn't* include my identity pattern in the recognition circuit?"

"In that case, you're no good to me, anyway," Mallon said flatly. "Two minutes—no more. Get going. And, just incidentally, if anything does go wrong, I'll cut the wench's throat, so help me."

I looked down at Renada, standing dazed at his side.

Would he? I found it hard to believe he would kill his precious pet to no purpose. On the other hand Tobey had more than proved he was as ruthless as he was crazy.

"Leave her alone, Tobey," I told him, "and I'll do it." He nodded lazily and I climbed over the improvised revetment.

I looked back at Mallon. He was old and shrunken in the garish light, his smooth gray suit rumpled, his thin hair mussed, the gun held in a white-knuckled grip. He looked more like a harassed shopkeeper than a would-be world-beater. Renada was still on her feet, a bit disheveled but still tall and lovely beside him, with Pig-Eye just behind, holding her arm.

"You must want the Bolo pretty bad to take the chance, Tobey," I said. "The girl's a stranger to me. I'll think about taking that wild shot; you can sweat me out . . ." I flipped slack into the wire trailing from my ankle and started across the weed-grown grass, a long black shadow stalking before me. The Bolo sat silent, as big as a bank in the circle of the spotlights. I could see the flecks of rust now around the ports and access covers, the small vines that twined up her sides from the ragged stand of weeds that marked no-man's-land.

Halfway there, and no gun ports had opened. The Bolo was ignoring me. So far, so good. It hadn't fired yet—so maybe I had a chance . . .

There was something white in the weeds ahead: broken human bones. I felt my stomach go rigid again. The last man had gotten this far; I wasn't in the clear yet . . .

I passed two more scattered skeletons in the next twenty feet. They must have come in on the run, guinea pigs to test the alertness of the Bolo.

Or maybe they'd tried creeping up, dead slow, an inch a day; it hadn't worked . . .

Tiny night creatures scuttled ahead, safe here in the shadow of the troll where no predator bigger than a mouse could move. I stumbled, diverted my course around a ten-foot hollow, the eroded crater of a near-miss. I wondered what kind of fighting had gone on here.

Now I could see the massive moss-coated treads, sunk six inches into the earth, the nests of field mice tucked in the spokes of the yard-high bogies. The quarter hatch was above, a hairline against the great curved flank. There were rungs set in the flaring tread shield. I reached up, got a grip, hauled myself up; my chain clanked against the metal. I found the door lever, held on, and pulled. It resisted, then yielded. From inside, there was the hum of a servo motor, a crackling of dead gaskets; the hairline widened, showing me a narrow companionway, green-anodized dural with black polymer treads, a bulkhead with a fire extinguisher, an embossed steel data plate that said BOLO DIVISION OF GENERAL MOTORS CORPORATION, and below, in smaller type, UNIT, COMBAT, BOLO MARK III, MODEL C.

The Great Troll was alive and ready to go, just sleeping. I pulled myself inside, went up into the Christmas-tree glow of instrument lights.

The control cockpit was small, utilitarian, with two deep-padded seats set among screens, dials, levers.

I sniffed the odors of oil, paint, the characteristic ether and ozone of a nuclear generator. There was a wavering hum in the air from idling relay servos. The clock showed ten past four. Either it was later than I thought, or the chronometer had gained in the last eighty-odd years. But I had no time to lose . . .

I slid into the seat, flipped back the cover of the command control console. The Cancel key was the big white one. I pulled it down and let it snap back, like a clerk ringing up a sale. A pattern of dots on the status display screen flicked out of existence. Mallon was safe from his pet troll now.

It hadn't taken me long to carry out my orders. I knew what to do next; I'd planned it all during my walk out. Now I had thirty seconds to stack the deck in my favor. I reached down, hauled the festoon of quarter-inch armored cable up in front of me. I hit a switch, and the inner conning cover—a disc of inch-thick armor—slid back. I shoved a loop of the flexible cable up through the aperture, reversed the switch. The cover slid closed again— and sliced the armored cable like overcooked macaroni, with only a few sparks.

I took a deep breath, and my hands went to the combat alert switch, hovered over it. It was the smart thing to do—the easy thing. All I had to do was punch a key, and the 9mm's would open up, scythe Mallon and his crew down like dead cornstalks—

But the scything would mow Renada down, along with the rest. And if I threw the Bolo in gear and drove off without firing, Mallon would probably keep his promise to cut that white throat . . .

My head was out of the noose now, but I would have to put it back—for a while.

I leaned sideways, reached back under the panel,

groped for a small fuse box. My fingers were clumsy. I took a breath, tried again. The fuse dropped out in my hand. The Bolo's sidescan was dead now. With a few more seconds to work, I could have knocked out other circuits—but my time had run out.

I grabbed the cut ends of my lead wire, knotted them around the chain for camouflage, and got out fast.

20

Mallon waited, crouched behind the revetment. The bodyguards and Renada weren't in sight.

"It's safe now, is it?" he grated, when I was beside him. I nodded. He stood, gripping his gun.

"Now we'll try it together," he growled, and motioned. "If you're lying, you'll get it, too." He grinned a nasty grin, and I went back over the parapet, Mallon right beside me with his gun ready. The lights followed us to the Bolo. Mallon clambered up to the open port, looked around inside, then dropped back down beside me. He looked excited now.

"That does it, Jackson. I've waited a long time for this. Now I've got all the *mana* there is!"

"Take a look at the cable on my ankle," I said softly. He narrowed his eyes, stepped back, gun aimed, darted a puzzled glance at the cable looped to the chain.

"I cut it, Tobey," I told him. "I was alone in the Bolo with the cable cut—and I didn't fire. I could have taken your toy and set up in business for myself, but I didn't."

Mallon paled, but recovered fast. "What's that supposed to buy you?" he rasped.

"As you said, we need each other. That cut cable proves you can trust me."

Mallon smiled. It wasn't a nice smile. "Safe, were you? Come here." I walked along with him to the back of the Bolo. A heavy copper wire hung across the rear of the machine, trailing off into the grass in both directions.

"I'd have burned you at the first move. Even with the other cable cut, I could have shunted the full load right into the cockpit with you. As soon as you touched metal—but don't be nervous. I've got other jobs for you." He jabbed the gun muzzle hard into my chest, pushing me back. "Now get moving," he snarled. "And don't ever threaten the Baron again."

Suddenly his tone changed. "You'll see how cracked I am, Whiz," he said, wheedling. "Stop fighting against it," he urged. "Join with me and we can have it all!"

"You could still launch *Prometheus*," I said. He looked at me as if he couldn't believe his ears.

"What?" he ground out. "Throw it all away? Waste all that the ship represents to send those fellows off on a meaningless mission? Think about it, Whiz! If—"

"Don't call me 'Whiz,' " I said. "Only my friends call me that."

He grabbed my arm. "I'm the best friend you could ever have," he told me. "I'm offering you half, Jackson, even now, with the job almost done . . ." He patted the corroding flank of the Great Troll. "I still mean to go through with my promise—not that I really promised you anything. Together we can wipe out Jersey and even Boston and Dee-

Cee, with a quick preemptive strike! We'll restore order; with our power plant in operation I estimate we can re-energize the power net all the way to the Mississippi! We'll be kings, Whiz, more than kings. We'll be the great benefactors of mankind! Surely you can see that?"

"They call it paranoia," I commented.

He laughed, a short bark. "You could be right," he cackled. "What's sane and what isn't? I've got a vision in my mind—and I'll make it come true. If that's insanity, it's better than what the mob has." He walked away from the Bolo; I trailed him, stepping over the bones.

Back at the parapet, Mallon stopped and turned to wait for me. "I've had my campaign planned in detail for years, Jackson. Everything's ready. I can move out, right on schedule, in half an hour—before any traitors have time to take word to my enemies. Pig-Eye and Dunger will keep you from being lonely while I'm away. When I get back—" He gestured and my whiskery friend and his sidekick loomed up, still dragging Renada.

"Let her go, Tobey," I said.

He gave me a parody of an astonished look, "In this condition? Nonsense, Whiz. That arm needs attention. I'll see to it promptly." He turned to his muscle-boys. "Watch him."

"Genghis Kahn is on the march, eh?" I said. "With nothing between you and the goodies but a five-hundred-ton Bolo . . ."

"The Lesser Troll . . ." He raised his hands and made crushing motions, like a man crumbling dry earth. "I'll trample it under my treads."

"You're confused, Tobey. The Bolo has treads; you just have a couple of fallen arches."

"It's the same," he said loftily. "I am the Great Troll!" He showed me a few stained teeth and walked away, leading Renada by her dislocated arm.

21

I moved along between Dunger and Pig-Eye toward the lights of the garage. Pig-Eye had a hand clamped on my arm.

"The back entrance again, and here I thought I was getting half the Kingdom," I said. "Anyone would think you were ashamed of me."

"You want more training, hah?" Dunger rasped. "Hold him, Pig-Eye." He unhooked his club and swung it loosely in his hand, glancing around. We were near the trees by the drive; there was no one in sight except the crews busy near the Bolo and a loose group by the front of the palace. Pig-Eye gave my arm a twist and shifted his grip to his old favorite stranglehold; I'd been hoping he would. Dunger whipped the club up, and I grabbed Pig-Eye's arm with both hands and leaned forward like a Japanese Admiral reporting to the Emperor. Pig-Eye went up and over just in time to catch Dunger's club across the back. He made a noise like a rusty spring. They went down together. I went for the club, but Whiskers was faster than he looked. He almost got a hand on it. I grabbed it and rolled clear, got to my knees, and laid it across his left arm, just below the shoulder. I heard the bone go . . . then I collapsed.

22

I remember falling; then I was back on my feet, unsteady but conscious. Pig-Eye lay sprawled. I heard him whining as though from a great distance. Dunger stood six feet away, the ring of black beard spread in a grin like a hyena smelling dead meat. His left arm dangled like a length of rope.

"His back's broke," he said. "Hell of a sound he's been making. I been waiting for you; I wanted you to hear it."

"I've heard it," I managed. My voice seemed to be coming off a worn soundtrack. "Surprised . . . you didn't work me over . . . while I was busy looking for my feet."

"Uh-uh. I like a man to know what's going on when I work him over." He stepped in carelessly, and I rapped the broken arm lightly with the club. Whiskers was tough; he choked the groan off in his throat. I backed a step without quite falling down, and he stalked me.

"Pig-Eye wasn't much, but he was my pal," Dunger told me. "Soon's I'm through with you, I'll have to kill him. A man with a broken back's no use to nobody. He'll be finished pretty soon now, but not you. You'll be around a long time yet; but I'll get a lot of fun out of you before the Baron gets back."

We were under the trees now. I wanted to lie down for a nice nap on the leaves; it must have showed. Dunger set himself and his eyes dropped to my belly. I didn't wait for it; I lunged at him. He laughed and stepped back, and my feet got tangled in those nice soft leaves, just enough to send me down. Dunger moved in. I got my legs under me and started to get up—

There was a hint of motion from the shadows behind Dunger. I shook my head to cover any expression that might have showed, let myself drop back.

"Don't try that old one on me, slave!" Dunger grated. "It hurts my feelings you think I'm that dumb!"

I let that one pass.

"Get up, damn you!" he snarled, and froze for an instant—then whirled. His hearing must have been as keen as a cat's; I hadn't heard a sound.

The old man stepped into view, right behind Dunger. His white hair was plastered to his skull, his big gnarled hands spread. Blood had run down from a wound on his scalp. Dunger snarled, jumped in and whipped the club up and down; I heard it hit. There was a flurry of struggle; then Dunger stumbled back, empty-handed.

I was on my feet again now. I made a lunge for Dunger just as he roared and charged. The club in the old man's hand rose and fell; Dunger crashed past him and blundered into the brush. The old man sat down suddenly, still holding the club. Then he let it fall and lay back. I went toward him, and Dunger rushed me from the side and we went down together. He got up.

23

I was dazed, but not feeling any pain now. Dunger had overdone it. He was standing over the old man. I could see the big lean body lying limply, face-upward, arms outspread. A bone handle protruded from the black blot on the front of the shabby mackinaw. The club lay on the ground a few feet away. I started crawling for it. It seemed a long way, and it was hard for me to move my legs, but I kept at it. The light rain was falling again now, hardly more than a mist. Far away there were shouts and the sound of engines starting up. Mallon's convoy was getting ready to move out. He had won. Dunger had won. The old man had tried, but it hadn't been enough. But if I could reach the club, and swing it just once . . .

Dunger was looking down at the old man. His back was to me. He leaned, withdrew the knife, wiped it on his trouser leg, hitching up his pants to tuck it away in its sheath. The club was smooth and heavy under my hand. I got a good grip on it, used it as a crutch to get to my feet. I waited until Dunger turned toward me, and then I hit him across the top of the skull with everything I had left . . .

24

I had thought the old man was dead until he moved suddenly. His features looked relaxed now, peaceful, the skin like parchment stretched over bone. I took his gnarled old hand and rubbed it. It was as cold as a drowned sailor.

"You waited for me, old timer?" I said inanely. He moved his head minutely, and looked at me. Then his mouth moved. I leaned close to catch what he was saying. His voice was fainter than lost hope.

"Mom . . . told me . . . wait for you . . . She said . . . you'd . . . come back some day . . ."

I felt my jaw muscles knotting. Inside me, something broke, and flowed away like molten metal. Suddenly my eyes were blurred—and not only with rain. I looked at the old face before me, and for a moment, I seemed to see a ghostly glimpse of another face, a small round face that had looked up at me . . .

He was trying to say something. I put my head down.

"Was I . . . a . . . good . . . boy . . . Dad?" Then his eyes closed. I sat for a long time, looking at the still face. Then I folded the hands on the chest and stood.

"You were more than a good boy, Timmy," I said. "You were a good man."

25

As soon as I was well clear of the palace grounds, I found a spot under a hedge out of the wind and stretched out to rest for a minute. I fell asleep instantly. My body had had enough exercise on no food and no rest. I woke up feeling better, though shivering. It wasn't really cold—in the sixties, maybe—but it was still dark. The lights in the hotel—oops, the palace—were back to normal. Probably Tobey's fury had burned itself out and Renada was back in the Baronial suite, catching up on her rest with no problem. In any event there was nothing I could do until things had calmed down—and I had healed up. All I could do for her now was get her killed.

I could see a faint glow in the sky to the west from the big town now, and there were tiny orange lights, probably from oil lamps, scattered medium-thickly down across the valley and in the area of Jasperton. Life went on, if not at the pre-collapse level, at least pretty generally.

I began for the first time to start thinking about what it was really like out there, how the survivors —or their descendants—were doing. Renada's folks, for example. I didn't really decide to go find out, I just found myself back on the road, headed for the nearest lights, which looked more like electric than oil. After a while I could hear the putt-putt of a generator motor.

I made my approach from off-road, threshing through the jimsonweeds that were busy reclaiming the acreage. I came to a rusty barbed-wire fence. The strands broke when I lifted them to duck under.

I froze where I was at a sound. It came again: a long-drawn-out groan, coming from the shadows under a big oak. I picked my way toward the sound, which was repeated over and over, with just enough interval for a labored breath, which I could also hear now.

I stopped and looked hard in the direction of the sound. A dim glow was coming from behind a jumble of planks. It didn't show me much, and there was no moon. I decided to risk using the flashlight, not forgetting to pat my .38 first, which I had found in Dunger's pocket, just to reassure the part of me that was saying "get the hell out of here and stick to your own problems."

The white beam showed me a sort of shelter made of rotted planks and dead branches up against the ruins of a concrete wall, with a piece of blue plastic sheet pulled over it. Below on the trampled ground lay a man dressed in clothes apparently tailored from an old canvas awning. His feet were bare, and I could see that one leg was twisted under him in a way no unbroken one could have managed. I put the light on his face for just an instant; all I saw was whiskers and a pair of small eyes that blinked in the light. He put an arm across his face and tried to say something, choked, coughed, spat, and said, "Douse that, Jasper!" He fumbled in the debris, and the glare-strip in the hut went off.

"You need help?" I asked him. His arm moved, groped feebly toward me.

"Hurt my laig some," he said.

I put the beam on the ground to pick my way over to him through a barrier of fallen branches. He was a heavy-set fellow of middle age. I could smell him at ten feet. I went around him to come up from the side, and as I stepped over him he whipped his arm over to grab my ankle in a grip like a power-clamp and jerk it from under me. I fell half across him, and his grip went instantly to my neck. I knocked his hand away, reached to recover the flashlight, and saw the legs of a second man, standing right in front of me. A rough voice said, "Look up, Sucky."

I kicked free of the grip and rolled over on my back; from here I could see the standing man, dressed in mangy, half-cured hides; he was taller and thicker than the other fellow, but just as whiskery. He had a round, blunt-featured face wearing a smile that had missed a lot of checkups. He held the grin, bent over and grabbed the light, flicked it around for a moment or two, then put it square on my face.

"This here's a Strangy, Raunch," he said. "Now," he went on, shifting his gaze to me; "what you want here, Strangy? No easy pickin's here fer sech as you."

"I heard him groaning," I told him, and under my coat I eased the .38 into my hand. "I thought he needed help."

"Oh, just one o' them Good Martians, huh?" he sneered. "Where was you headed on the strip yonder?"

The silence was absolute, an aching void of noiselessness, not even any groaning. I looked over at Whiskers Number One. He was sitting up, groping around in the litter. He saw me watching him, and reached to yank his twisted leg from under him and pull up the ragged-edged cuff, giving me a glimpse of a shiny metal rod in place of a shin. He carelessly flipped the hinged rod out straight and got to his feet.

"Titanium," he commented. "Better'n the old one."

"What for?" I wondered aloud. "Why me?"

"First let's see what you got on you," he said and took a step toward me. I showed him the revolver pointed at his gut and told him to stay where he was. I motioned to Number Two, but he grinned and took a long step toward me. "Hell, Raunch," he said. "He ain't got none o' them bullets for that thang."

I squeezed and put one into the weathered plank beside him. Both of them were staring at me with their mouths open. Number Two had one black tooth, just off-center on top.

"What was the idea of baiting me in here?" I asked them. "Traffic couldn't be very heavy here; you were waiting for me."

"Orders," Raunch mumbled. "But they didn't say nothing about no magic stuff, like that daylight-stick, and the bang-thing."

"A pistol, Raunch," the other fellow corrected contemptuously. "Don't give the stranger here the idea we're ignorant rubes."

"I asked a question," I reminded the gabby one. "What did you want with me?"

"Oh, it ain't *you*," he assured me. "It's what you got on you—like that pistol and the flashlight. We ain't all dumb's Raunch here." He held out a dirty and heavily callused hand. "You ain't got a chance, Strangy," he said comfortably. "Better hand it over and maybe I'll go light on you cause you didn't know no better."

I answered with another round, this one close enough to send wood splinters into his shin. He yelped and grabbed at his leg to cover his lunge toward me. I aimed carefully and fired into the folds of the greasy furs. He yelled and fell backwards. Lying there, his little pig eyes glaring at me, he ran through an inventory of obscenities that included a couple I'd never heard before.

I yawned and took aim at his nose and said, "Shut up, Dum-dum, or I'll let some fresh air into your IQ."

Behind me, Raunch laughed. "Old Walt ain't got none," He said between guffaws. "Serve the mother right."

I moved over to where I could cover both of them. "Plug the hole," I told Raunch. "He's not hurt; just a broken rib or two, maybe."

"I'm hurt bad," Walt groaned and cuffed Raunch when he leaned over to examine the wound. Raunch kicked him in his good ribs and said, "You're mixed up, Walt-boy. It's you's flat on yer back; I'm standing. You got any sense you'll be nice, now."

"Help me, Raunchy!" Walt began babbling and threw open the moldy dog-hide coat to expose a surprising amount of blood and an expanse of dirty hide with a ragged gouge with white bone splinters. Raunch shuddered and said, "Why, Walty, that ain't no more'n a scratch." He poked the purple-black bruise around the wound and grinned when Walt yelled, "Easy, Raunchy!"

"You can count on it!" Raunch said cheerfully; he spat on a wad of grass and started dabbing at the blood with it. I watched as Walt's hand groped out into a small heap of trash, while he bucked and humped to cover the move.

"Why, Walt, that don't hurt none," Raunch told him. He was still grinning when the length of rusted iron impacted his skull with a squishy sound. Walt pushed the corpse aside and got grotesquely to his knees and looked up at me.

"It's you and me now, partner," he told me. "Without me you won't get nowhere, wherever yer goin'. You got the stuff and I got the know-how." He thrust out a grimy, thick-fingered hand. "Jest gimme a hand up here," he was rattling on. "I'll show you where some stuff is stashed'll put us in good with the Man, old pal."

I managed to resist the temptation to be pals with Walt, and his swipe with the rusty bar missed by a good inch when I stepped back instead of into it. Walt chuckled and wiped his mouth with the back of his hand.

"Hadda make sure you wasn't too dumb to depend on," he told me in a confidential, between-pals tone.

"Who do you work for, Dum-dum?" I asked him.

"You got me wrong, pal," he whined. "Old Dum-dum's on post yonder," he tilted his shaggy head

to indicate the direction of the nearest cluster of
yellow lights—the same ones I'd been headed for.

"Naw," he shook his head, rejecting my wrong
ideas. "Me and old Raunch there, we split off on
our own here Monday a week. Got the line on the
stuff, see, from some poor sucker wanted us to go
in with him. Said he found it when he was shopping over the Mall."

"Tell me about it," I ordered. He had worked
his way forward while my attention was distracted
by his shrewd conversation. I told him to drop the
iron bar and he put it down tenderly, well within
reach.

"Said it was magic stuff," Walt scoffed. "Electronics supplies most likely. Man like you'd know
what to do with it."

"You don't believe in magic?" I queried, hefting
the pistol.

"Oh, Lordy yes, sir!" he hastened to assure me.
"I mean I know it works, OK, but *believe* in it?
Hell, I know it's what they call 'science' and all. I
put in my time yonder in the palace," he added in
explanation.

"Why'd you leave?" I wondered aloud.

"Same's you, most likely," he grunted and gained
another inch closer to both me and the bar. "Had
my eye on the Mall a long time," he confided.
"Figgered a man could pretty well set up in the
baron business, he had all that stuff. If that mark
we closed down could get in, so can we."

"He told you how before you killed him?" I
asked.

Walt spat. "I watched the sucker come out—
like we done you. We got all the routes covered.
Seen how he done it; we can go in the same way."

"What do you think is in there?" I demanded, and jabbed the pistol toward him when he hesitated. He jumped and, miming startlement, got a hand on the bar.

"Gee, sir," he whined. "Reckon ever'body knows that, no disrespect intended, sir." He was getting his legs under him. I shot the bar out of his hand as if casually. He howled and slung his fingers, then jammed them into his mouth.

"That smarted some, sir," he moaned.

"Nothing like one in the kneecap would," I said. "But we're pals, remember?" I mocked him. "You weren't really thinking about using that on me, were you, Dum-dum?"

"Naw," he averred with a throwing-away motion that put his hand within twelve inches of it. "You can trust me, sir," he said wheedlingly. "You and me, we can have it all, sir. I *need* you and I know it, and *you* need me." He looked as satisfied as a bundle of whiskers with a red-rimmed hole in it can look.

"What're the lights over there?" I asked him.

"Oh, *them* lights. The Settlement; Old Bunny's place. Thinks he's smart, Old Bunny. Got that there Briggs goin', tried to put me to work. Me! Do slave work fer Bunny!" He paused to show me the black stump in his inflamed gums. "That's a good one," he chuckled. "Them bodyguards o' his: one of em tried to git in my way." Walt's voice had gone dreamy. "I bent him some before I taken off, you bet. Got even for a lot, that time," he added contentedly, and leaned sideways just far enough to try a leg sweep that didn't quite work out. I lined my sights squarely on his mouth. "I might as well do it now," I told him. "I'll have to eventually, anyway."

He yawned, a gape big enough to engulf a small chicken, whole, and got to his feet, wincing a little as he straightened up his thick torso. He made a production of tucking up his bloody furs, turned his back to me and said. "Go ahead, Strangy, only you won't." He had taken a step; now he turned to face me. "That's why your kind can never win," he sneered. "You know damn well I'll skull you first chance I get, but you can't do nothing about it. You *can't*, Strangy! Go ahead, make a liar outa me."

I shifted my aim to his crotch and put one through the inside of his thigh. He exploded backward with a yowl that made his earlier efforts seem like the chirp of a baby bird. He went down, threshing in the leaf-litter, rolled right over the bar, which somehow wasn't there after he rolled clear.

" 'Thou shalt not kill' doesn't mean 'thou shalt not have a little fun,' " I told him. "If you happen to lose a little too much blood, that's your look-out."

"Ye'r a mean man," he grieved. "Message said—" He interrupted himself to pull back his clothing to take a look at the hole. There was plenty of blood, but I'd been careful to miss the femoral artery. He wiped his sleeve over the wound, then grabbed up some dirt and used it to plug the hole. Maybe he figured his tetanus shots were up-to-date.

"That's enough clowning," I said. "Now get over there and lay Raunch out nicely, and then lie down beside him."

He started to gobble. "Look at my pal Raunch,

with his brains on his face. *You* done that! I can
eyewitness testify! Old Bunny sees this, he'll have
a rope on you before you can say, 'Jake Rubinstein'!"

I kicked him in the shin and he started crawling
toward the dead man. As soon as he was within
reach, he began rifling the corpse, fumbling bits of
trash—a button, a rusty jackknife, some mushy
stuff that might once have been a hard-boiled egg—
into his own baggy pockets. I leaned over to crack
him lightly on the head with the pistol muzzle,
but he hardly noticed.

"Skunk was holding out on me," he remarked in
a shocked tone, and held up a dime-store ring
with a red glass gem. He tried it on his hand,
finally got it over the tip of his little finger. I
reminded him of his instructions, and he switched
off the chatter and said aggrievedly, "I was *going*
to!"

I spent another ten mintues trying without much
luck to convince Walt that he'd lost this one. I
finally had to knock him down and tie him to a
couple of small saplings with some still-fresh nylon
line I found in the falling-down hut. He expressed
his disapproval, so I went back and arranged Raunch
beside him.

"Hey, you ain't going to leave me here like
this!" he yelled, pulling as far from the body as his
bonds allowed.

"He won't start smelling real bad for about three
days," I reassured him. "By then you won't care."

"Shoot me with that there fire-gun," he moaned.
"Get it over quick. Come on, Strangy, give a
feller a break."

I looked down at him sternly. "Listen to yourself, Dum-dum," I ordered. "You're begging me to kill you. Don't you get it, yet? It means this is one time your lying and trickery won't work. Now, you and your buddy set out to victimize, preferentially, anyone who tried to help you. Nice fellows: not content to just scrag some innocent bypasser, you wanted to kill someone who still had a human impulse to help a fellow human in pain. Okay, the fun's over now. I suggest you yell until your throat bleeds, then fight that nylon until your wrists are raw, then hit yourself in the head with that axle-shaft you've so cleverly slipped up your sleeve. You'll have to hold it in your gums, of course. Ta."

I walked away toward the lights and to my disgust felt my damned conscience bothering me. But to hell with that; I had one Bunny to contend with next. But it wasn't quite that simple, as I should have expected. I heard the *pop*! of a twig off to my left in the scrub woods, and my body hit the deck with no need for instructions. Something whistled over me and hit in the weeds and went skittering away. I rolled toward the direction of the pop and the missile had come from and saw him silhouetted against the faint glow of the eastern sky. My God! It was almost daylight already!

I had a lot of work to do before I could afford to walk around in broad daylight—but I wouldn't have to worry about walking around if the new boy got a better bead next time. I could see the short, thick, recurved bow in his hands. He was fitting another arrow to it. I could see the big triangular hunting-point from here. I waited until he had the arrow set and was aiming in my general direction, looking for that telltale hint of motion; then I put

the round into the wide part of the grip. The bent
bow exploded in his hands and he staggered back,
bleating.

"All right, Cupid," I yelled. "Come on over
here, slow and easy. Don't try to do anything
smart; you're not equipped for it."

He was smart enough to follow orders. He seemed
to have trouble seeing his way; he blundered into
a tree and batted clumsily at a low branch that
wouldn't get out of his way. I put the light on his
face: it was a bloody mess. He kept pawing at his
eyes.

"Keep your hands off your face," I told him.
"Move to your left, now." I got my feet under me,
put the light away and got the old revolver back in
my hand. I had one round left. He came up,
puffing hard and making a thin whining sound. I
told him to sit down on his hands and lie back on
the leaf-mold. He muttered, but did as he was
ordered. I flicked the light across his face and
shuddered.

"I'm going to look at your face," I told him.
"That doesn't mean it would be a good time to try
something. The pistol will be aimed at your heart."
I prodded his chest, somewhere under a heap of
flea-infested fur, *à la* Walt. I had the light in my
teeth, and aimed it at his face. At first all I saw
was a cluster of splinters projecting from bloody
meat. There was a glint of white eyeball in there
somewhere. I studied the eye. Aside from small
splinters puncturing the eyelid, it looked intact. I
said, "Hold still," and began pulling them out.
They came easily, and after I'd removed a dozen
or so I said, "Blink your eye."

"I cain't!" he yelled. "I'm blind!" Then he shut up and blinked open and shut half a dozen times.

"That feels better, Strangy," he commented. "Not good, but better. "Now, you just pull a few more—here, I'll hold that fire-gun fer you, so's you can work better."

I jabbed the barrel harder into his ribs and brushed aside his hand which had moved up, ready to claim the weapon, an indication of his profound conviction that kindness was stupidity, and that I'd hand over the gun on command.

"I can always ram one back in, right square in the middle of the pupil," I reminded him. "Forget your ideas for the moment."

"Oh, Hickey," Walt's voice sounded mournfully from his spot in the shadows. "Hurry up, Hick! 'Fore he puts one over on you. You oughta see what he done to our ol' pal Raunch: busted his head, he done!"

"I seen it, Walt," my patient called. "*You* busted him."

"I never," Walt wailed. "We was waiting here, meant to ask the Strangy did he need any he'p, and he up and whopped old Raunch!"

"Shut up," I told Hicky before he could reply. I removed a few more splinters from the vicinity of his eye; then I stood up. He scrambled to his feet and took a step toward Walt and Raunch before I said, "Hold it right there." He hesitated for a moment, then took another step.

"Got to see to ol' Walt," he said as one stating the obvious.

I told him to turn around and he did.

"You can pick out the rest of 'em now," I told

him. He reached to his eye, felt around gingerly, selected the biggest shard of wood and yanked it free, uttering a yelp as he did so.

"I'm hurt bad," he offered. "Can see some, but not good. Man can't see good ain't got a chance."

"Man talks too much makes my finger itch," I replied.

"Reckon I better get back." He began to edge off to his left, toward the lights. "Got to get he'p," he explained. He was still sure he was dealing with a moron.

"You move again before I tell you and I'll put one in your knee," I told him. He looked around as if listening for some expected sound, such as the arrival of reinforcements. I motioned him over to the sagging boards of the collapsing hut.

"Switch on the light," I told him.

"Lordy, Strangy, I can't do that." He sounded shocked, but he reached in under a plank, and the battery-fed glare-strip came feebly to life. "Lie down," I ordered. He looked down at the trash underfoot and said, "Where at?" then tossed aside a few rusty cans.

I went over and picked up one of the loops of rusty wire I'd noticed and told him to put his hands behind his back with his wrists crossed. He began to bluster, then shut up when I kicked him hard in the shin. When he had his grimy wrists crossed, I wired them that way. He started to whine, making a big show of trying to pull free.

"Hurts, Strangy!" he stated. "Hurts bad! Can't reach my face now where it itches me bad and hurts, too! Cut me loose, Strangy! I'm suffer'n'!" He did a stage fall and rolled on his back. I stepped around out of kick-range, and stood over him, studying what I could see of his whiskery, dirt-crusted, bloody face. It had never been pretty, alas. His expression was half crafty, half that of a crying baby.

"You're an interesting case, Hickey," I told him. "You truly believe that the fact that I helped you, and incidentally kept you from blinding yourself rubbing those splinters into your eye, proves that I'm weak in the head. You're not just stalling; you actually believe I'm so dumb I'll turn you loose so you can take another try at killing me."

"Naw, nothing like that, Strangy," he came back, dropping the crying-baby part of his routine. "Lissen, you need me, feller, you plan to kill old Bunny. See, I know how to get past them guards o' his and all. So cut me loose and let's get started!"

"Oh, did I want to kill Bunny?" I inquired inter-estedly. "Why was that, do you suppose? Who is he, anyway?"

"You ain't got to be cagey with me, feller," he confided. "I had in mind to kill him my own self," this last as one revealing a valuable secret.

"I'd never have guessed."

He nodded vigorously. "Fact," he confirmed. "See, he taken my fort, my women, coupla brats I was he'pin even, slaves, supplies, the whole works! Done it by tricks, see, taken advantage of my good nature and all." He paused, as if contemplating the iniquities of humanity. "Swored I'd get him," he added, nodding in agreement with himself. "Jest waiting fer the right time, was all. Now I see the time's here!" He spat off to one side and shot a look at me to see how I was taking it.

I spat in the same direction. "You're a comical cuss, Hickey," I told him, and backed away a step. I glanced over toward where Walt was resting quietly, beside Raunch, who was even quieter. Hickey was struggling to his feet. I let him.

"What we got to do," he went on, encouraged by my carelessness, closing the deal while the sucker was still carried away by his eloquence, "we got to set far to this here post. Better drag them two over here where it'll burn hot, with the shack and all." He kicked idly at the leaf-litter and moldering planks scattered around. "Burn good," he predicted, "you and me, we barely got clear, tried to save them two boys but couldn't. No, wait!" he interrupted himself as inspiration took hold. "I got an even *better* plan: They'll come a running, see, to try to save the shack and all, and you and me, we'll lie low yonder." He pointed with his ear toward the nearest outthrust tongue of scrub oak. "Pick 'em off two at a time and get us some good weepons that way, see?" He poked out a thick pink tongue to touch his overly red lips in anticipation of the fun. "Just get me unwired here is all," he added as an afterthought, and turned his back to me so I could get at the wire, a little bloody from his theatrics.

I picked up a foot-long twig and reached out to touch his wrist with it, and he spun like a spring-loaded door, closer, doing a nice leg-sweep that only missed me by two feet. The momentum dumped him back on his sore face. He yelped and then looked up at me, all crafty now. I looked back at him without approval.

"You're one of those slow learners you hear

about," I remarked. "Try, Hickey, *try* to get an idea into that hairball you use for a brain: you don't get to eat me for dinner. True, I was dumb enough to try to help a wounded man, but I'd sour on your stomach. Clear?"

"Aw, feller, you ain't going to count that one? I was jest funnin' ya," he essayed without much enthusiasm. "Hark!" His eyes went wide and he cocked his head, miming alertness. "Hush, now," he decreed, and made a flattening motion with his hands. "Git down! Won't do to have old Bunny find us here like this. But you do like I say and we can get clear." He raised his voice. "I tol' ya I'm taking you in to the Man!" Then in a whisper: "Strangy, you got to help me! If Bunny gets aholt of me, he'll gut me on that altar o' his!"

"Help you how, you treacherous scum?" I asked him. He made *shush*ing motions and hissed. "Keep it down! Ol' Bunny can hear like a bat! Reason he got the name Bunny; big ears, get it?"

I acknowledged that I got it and added that I still didn't quite see why he thought I'd give him another chance to kill me. He twisted his ugly face and whispered, "Naw, all that was before, 'fore I knew how sharp you was, fella. Had to be sure I could trust you not to foul up 'fore I went and told you about the treasure." He was still offering his tied wrists expectantly.

About then, I heard a twig *pop!* off in the darkness to the left. Up until then I'd thought it was just another of Hickey's little games. I didn't want to meet Mister Bunny this way any more than he did. "Get down!" I told Hickey, and he knelt and then went down flat on his face in the ground-litter.

I eased back against the only tree in the trampled area and froze. There was someone not ten feet away, coming silently around the end of the broken planks of the collapsed hut. I felt the broken stave of Hickey's bow under my foot, and stooped to investigate; the string, nylon apparently, was intact. The stave was in two equal-length pieces. All the damage was in the grip area. I flexed one of the halves, which felt like a laminated affair of wood and horn layers. It still had plenty of spring. I looped the string in one notch and tied the other end around the shattered grip, then felt around for the arrows Hickey had dropped. I found one, nocked it, and, by raising it far enough to silhouette it against the pre-dawn sky, could see it well enough to aim more or less toward the pocket of dense shadow where our visitor was biding his time. I let fly and got a *thump!* and a yelp, quickly muffled.

Hickey came to his knees and scrambled over that way. I heard sounds I decided were better not investigated and saw the outline of the second man as he moved sidways, around behind the shack. Then there was whispering.

I waited, getting another arrow ready. There were threshing sounds and Hickey came back, crawling awkwardly on his knees with his hands still behind him. I stayed glued to my tree. When he reached the spot where he'd seen me last, he fell forward, and I got a glimpse of his barely visible wrists; they were free. He put them back in place as if they were still bound and said, "I got the sumbitch. Old Picky, tryna pull a fast one.

Even warred up like you done me, I got him! Now we got to . . ." His voice trailed off.

I could see that he was looking around, trying to locate me. I tossed a pebble behind him and his hand struck out, light glinting on the knife in his fist. He grunted when he found no target waiting and snarled, "Whereat *are* ye, pal?"

I ignored him and turned my attention to the other one coming around the hut, making a little sound now, just a bit careless. I could have nailed him, but I lay low and kept my makeshift bow aimed. The brush was high and thick at the right-hand end of the ruined shack: the latrine area, probably. I saw the bushes shake and a hand groped into view. The visibility was getting better fast. The hand that was feeling over the trash on the ground was small, almost delicate. I managed to ease around closer to the new arrival, who had withdrawn the hand now, and a head of long hair with a dirty ribbon appeared.

"Hold it right there," I told her. She looked toward my voice and waited. She was no beauty. About a tough forty, I estimated, with blunt features, a nose and lips that had been flattened and split, like one of those slum boys in the prelims who thought he could fight. She brushed a leaf away from her face and said, "Hickey, you all right?"

"Hickey's not all right, sister. The deal went sour. Now you come out where I can see you."

She pushed through the screen of overgrown jimsonweed on all fours and peered in my direction, trying to see who she was talking to. "You don't dare shoot off that far-gun again," she said in

a conversational tone. Her voice was throaty but
not sexy. "Maybe we could work something out,
Strangy," she offered. "You know dern well I got
no cause to favor Bunny none."

"The name is Lieutenant Commander Jackson,"
I told her. For some reason I was tired of being
called "Strangy."

"Hell, I'm Admiral Betsy Black," she came back.
"So what? Reckon them fancy titles don't cut much
stuff out here."

"Why are you creeping around this dump in the
dark, Admiral?" was my next attempt.

"See who's down here, shootin off the far-gun,"
she told me matter-of-factly. "Not many'd waste
the magic thataway."

"How many are with you?" I demanded.

"Only old Picky over there; Hickey cut Picky's
neck pretty good, after Picky unwarred him. Not
too smart, Picky wasn't."

"Hickey conned him, eh?"

"Conned him, hell," she scoffed. "He cut his
throat with his own knife, soon's he got a hand
loose."

"And then he was to keep me occupied while
you did the sneak around right end, eh?" I
prompted.

She shook her head. "Claimed you was pals.
Said he could put the knife into yer neck fore you
seen he wasn't warred up no more."

"He missed that one," I told her.

"Too bad," she commiserated. "And you pals,
too."

"Look, Betsy," I tried. "I need information.
Maybe you'd be willing to help me."

"What makes you think so?" she asked. "Old Hickey told me and Picky about you, 'fore Pick's throat got cut thataway. Come up quiet, saying' how he got away to warn us; you was a bad un, shot Walt with that fire-gun whilst he was trying to he'p you." She paused to let that sink in. "Said where he'd sneak back and sucker you—only way we could stop ya from shooting the three of us. Got pore dumb Picky to unwar him—I told him doncha do it, but by then Hickey was loose and got Picky's sticker and cut him from ear to ear. Plumb ugly sight, what I could see of it. But I come on around, see what you looked like—can't see good, but I know I never seen you before. Who are you, feller?" She gave me a keen look. "You must be Tary," she told me. "I'm Tary, too," she added, sounding proud, then she got back to business. "Reckon Walt and Raunch caught you coming from the palace yonder. You must be one o' the Baron's bunch, eh? No disrespect, Lootenant."

" 'Lieutenant Commander,' " I corrected her. "Yes, I came from the palace, but I'll be candid with you: I'm *not* one of his bunch."

"What's that 'candid'?"

I told her to skip it. "I've been out of touch," I said. "I need to know the situation out here in the countryside. So how about briefing me?"

"Things is bad," she said. "All right if we set? I'm tarred." We fixed up a couple of planks across some broken concrete blocks, and I turned up a chipped and faded enameled sign that read BOB'S EXXON.

I had a sudden *déjàvu*: a small, neat convenience store *cum* service station, a couple of miles out on State 39. I do mean "service"; Bob used to come out and pump gas and check the oil and wipe the windshield. I used to go out of my way to go there—here—because I had a bellyfull of watching other gas pump jockeys sitting inside out of the drizzle, doing nothing, while nicely-dressed young service wives got out of their cars and got their pretty hands greasy checking their own oil, at a price that was high enough to pay for hand-dipping with a silver teaspoon. Hard to make a connection between Bob's immaculate little square of lawn with rosebeds and this patch of trash and weeds. No matter: that was then and this was now, and a world had collapsed in the interval.

"Tell me about it," I urged her. "Is it all anarchy? Has the country been invaded? Is there still a president and an Armed Forces?"

"I don't know nothing about none of that stuff," she told me, with an almost Chaucerian disregard for the multiplicity of negatives. "Not enough eats," she went on. "Not enough dry places to sleep, and ever'body fights over what there is, nacherly, 'cept when Bunny's around. That what you mean?" she queried abruptly. "Like you was jest in from Mars?"

I nodded. "Exactly, Betsy," I said encouragingly. "How long has it been like this?" it occurred to me to ask her.

She shook her head. "Always, I reckon," she answered. "Least as long's I been alive. Heard some old folks once, said things use to be better, all the magic stuff useta work, they said. Prolly jest yarning, you know how old folks are."

"No, tell me, how are they?" I pressed her.

"Dead, mostly," she told me without emphasis.

"You know, they get where they can't work no more, can't even do fer theirselfs, got to take 'em out, leave 'em for the dogs."

"Nice," I commented. "Same for anybody foolish enough to get sick, or born?"

"Sure," she confirmed without hesitation. "I got all's I can do to keep myself fed. Where'm I gonna get eats to give to some sprat some sloppy female done throwed?"

"Good question," I agreed. "Where *do* you get your eats?"

"Don't go prying, trying to fox me, Mister," she reprimanded me sharply. "Ever'body's got his own stock someplace. Heard even this post here had some good stuff once." She looked at what was left of Bob's tidy little store. "What about you, feller? What you doing out here? Bunny and them heard the fire-guns over headquarters, seen lights and figgered might somebody come along this way. Why old Walt and Raunch was posted out here. I and Pick come along when we heard the fire-gun close-like. Better move along soon, I reckon." She changed the subject sharply. "Better get clear. Bunny don't like finding his troops kilt like that." She nodded toward where Walt and Raunch lay in an untidy heap.

"Walt's not dead," I told her.

"Why not?" she came back, sounding disgusted. "You saving him for a special occasion, or what?"

"It wasn't necessary. He's immobilized. That's good enough."

"So he'll lay there and starve if the dogs don't find 'im first," she said to herself. She shot me a guarded look. It was getting light enough to see now.

"You're right about getting out of here. Nothing I've heard about this Bunny makes me want to meet him at a disadvantage."

"Don't know where that 'disavage' is at," she grumped, "But we can hide out over the plant, yonder." She flicked her uncombed head indicating "west." I tried hard to make the connection between the wilderness I was standing in and the view along 39. I remembered the new assembly plant over that way, one of those Japanese-American joint ventures, supposed to bring two thousand new jobs to Jasperton. There were no lights over that way now.

"What's there?" I asked her. She twisted her face and said, "Stuff. No eats; lots of metal, though. Hey, where you from, feller? You one o' them plane folks from over Lanster?"

I shook my head. "Never mind, Admiral; it's a long story."

"Thought you might be," she explained. "You look like you's fed good and all. Cept one o' them fellers wouldn't have no fire-gun or be by hisself."

I waved a hand. "All this used to be farms, as neat as a Jaycee's desk. All the machines used to work: cars and electric gadgets. People lived in nice houses and kept a dog as a pet. What happened?"

She hunkered down on her hard haunches and it was her turn to shake her head. " 'Fore my time," she grunted indifferently. "Heard tell about how thangs useta be. Then somethin' went wrong. Dunno what." She looked around as if for a clue she hadn't previously noticed. "Been in the town yonder." She nodded in the direction of Jasperton. "Wonder why folks'd live that close together, no bars on the windows. Seen all them awe-mobiles. Nigh ever house had one, seems like. Ugly things. Wondered what they was for. Heard they useta move around and folks could get on and ride; seen they's seats inside some of em. Don't b'lieve that stuff. And hows come they's so many of 'em?"

"The land was valuable," I told her. "So the builders squeezed as many houses as they could onto the land they owned. People needed the cars to get to work, or the store, or visit their friends, go to shows, or just ride in the country."

"Aw, yer foolin' me, Strangy. I don't know a whole lot, but you saying' folks *owned* the land, like it was somethin' they made or scrounged? That's pretty silly, feller. And I never seen no dead horse remains, so how'd these here cars go? You ain't telling me they was alive and could go on their own?"

"They have engines," I said without much enthusiasm. "Like Bunny's Briggs, only bigger."

She got to her feet. "You know, ye'r a terrible liar. I ain't dumb, just iggorant. Can't no pile o' arn that size go noplace."

"What about the wheels?" I suggested. "The wheels show they were meant to move."

"Why, three men can't hardly push one! Wheels is all flat on the bottom side. Don't move easy. Ever try to push one o' them thangs, feller?"

"They'll go close to a hundred miles an hour. That was when the roads were good, of course." I nodded toward the potholed highway barely visible through the tall weeds.

"You mean the strip?" she asked. "What you mean 'good'?"

"They were called roads," I told her. "And a good road is smooth, no potholes or cracks. Most of 'em had lights on them, and painted lines to keep you in your lane, and signs beside them to give you information. There were gas stations and motels and restaurants whenever you needed one. One of our best things. Never before and never again will humanity have a system like that." I heard myself getting preachy. "They cut right through wilderness and mountains and across swamps and rivers, connected every town with every other town."

"Naw." She dismissed my lecture. "Nobody'd spend all that time on something you don't have no use for."

"They were used plenty."

"Couldn't 'a' done anyways," she went on, ignoring me. "You ever feel how hard that there strip is? No way nobody's going to find all that hard stuff right in a line that way."

"They *put* it there!"

"Quit try'n'a kid me, Strangy. I wasn't borned day 'fore yestiddy."

I was trying to place her dialect, without much luck. It was all-American, but seemed to be a mixture of rural and big-city patois, with a few trimmings of her own.

"Where *were* you born, Admiral?" I asked her.

She waved her arm. "Yonder, of course," she snapped in a tone that was impatient with foxy strangies.

"What's 'yonder' mean in this context?" I pressed her.

"The Settlement," she grunted. "Couldn't hardly be borned noplace else. Where the shelter is at."

"I didn't know."

"You don't know much," she grumped. "Can't figger you, Strangy. Never kilt old Walt and Hickey, nor even Picky. Funny. Aint' kilt me, neither," it occurred to her. "What you expect to get from me? You ain't after my bod," she conceded, looking herself over appraisingly. "Never *was* purty. Now I'm old, I ain't even trade goods. What you want, keepin' me alive?"

"You sound as if you want me to shoot you," I suggested.

"Hell, no, Strangy. I got a lot o' life in me yet. Know plenty, too. You need me, feller, that's why you ain't kilt me yet." She looked at me with what seemed to be a hopeful expression.

I grinned at her quite spontaneously. She grinned back for a moment, then it faded.

"Making faces don't change nothing," she reprimanded me sharply.

"What's to change?" I wanted to know. "You came sneaking around here to kill me, according to your own story," I pointed out. "I didn't give you the chance, and we've been pumping each other. Where do we go from here?"

She looked puzzled, and scratched at her rump as if in confirmation, then got thoughtful for a moment. "About them strips: Where was all them folks going, huh?" Now she seemed smug, as if she'd scored a point.

"To work," I said, "home, on vacation, to visit, deliver goods, or sometimes just for fresh air."

She was dubious. "Plenty o' work to do at home, I reckon. What's that 'ivasion' yer said about?"

" 'Vacation.' It means the time you take off from your regular work to get a change of scene, do something for fun."

"Why would anybody be willing to get kilt just to change the scene, like you said?" she challenged me promptly. "And what's this 'fun'?"

I tried to tell her. "It's anything you do that you enjoy, get pleasure from; something you like to do for its own sake."

"Oh." She nodded. "Like shooting old Walt and Raunch yonder with that fire-gun."

"I didn't," I repeated. "Go look; Walt's not dead, and Raunch got brained *by* Walt."

She rose. "All right, Strangy," she said, sounding tired. "I guess you mean it. But I can do it if you can't."

"Do what?" I asked unnecessarily.

"Kill the mother." She stated the obvious.

"Why?"

"Fer that 'fun' you was saying about," she told me impatiently.

"No," I said.

She gave me an astonished look. "Looky, feller, I'm not plannin' on havin' old Walt come back and jump me in the dark. If he ain't dead he heard ever'thang I been telling you."

"Why you and not me?"

"Now they know you're too skeered to do it, they won't care nothing about *you*, one way or another," she informed me soberly.

"How many people live over there?" I asked, indicating the half-mile-distant lights of the Settlement.

She tossed her head in a vague gesture. "Oh, Bunny got maybe this many top boys," she stated, holding up both hands, fingers spread.

"Only ten?" I mumbled.

"Top boys, that is," she repeated. "Go another" —she opened and closed her hands twice—"slaves. Got the females, o' course, and a few o' their sprats."

"He doesn't like kids?"

"Who does? Gettin' 'em hurts like hell, from the yells I hear. Then all they is is trouble. Dirt comin' outa one end and noise outa the other. Keep the ma's workin' the whole time, use up good eats, do nothin'."

"So Bunny doesn't like having them around."

"Feeds 'em to the pigs, mostly," she snorted. "Pigs love 'em. That what you call a sack of flies, to Basser-Sumbish—the Swine God." She paused, then added, "Saves carryin' slop, too. Other ones stay in the shelter," she added, by the way.

"What about the future? Who's going to carry on the town when you and Bunny and his top hands and slaves are gone?"

"Who cares?" She showed me her amazed look again. "I'm daid, what difference it gonna make to me?"

"I suppose that's one way of looking at it," I conceded.

She said, "Hell! You telling me you're interested in what's gonna happen after you're dead?"

"Yes, I am."

"Why?" was her next question.

I thought about it. "I don't really know," I had to admit. "I suppose part of it is concern for the world my kids are going to live in."

She turned to give me a hot look. "You claim you made some o' them sprats?" she snapped. "Hell, even if you did, how'd anybody ever know? Who, I mean?"

"Things were different when I grew up," I told her. "How about you? You were a sprat yourself once."

She spat. "You got no call to go talking nasty," she told me. "I been nice, ain't I?"

"You haven't given me a straight answer yet," I pointed out.

"You ain't said where you're from, neither, Strangy," she riposted. "You ain't no Baron's man. I seen them before. Beat you up first and talk after."

"I come from a strange place called the United States, that nobody cared enough about to defend. It wasn't perfect, by any means," I conceded, "but we could have perfected it."

"I heard about that 'Nice Day,' " she told me. " 'Oz,' too; 'Fairyland.' No such places. Folks all going around doing things fer one 'nother, don't make sense. Never could figger it." She held up one combat-booted foot. "Like these here shoes," she went on. "Found a place full of 'em—all sizes. Now, who went and collected all them shoes? Couldn't nobody wear more'n one size. And the eats; in them little square caves-like. Whyn't whoever put it there eat it hisself? All kinds o' stuff. Taken some work to cure them hides and make them shoes. What fer?"

"It was called 'society,' " I said. "It took our ancestors fifty thousand years to develop it, one painful step at a time. Then we threw it away."

"Now I know ye'r foolin' me. Nobody don't know nothin' about what happened fifty thousand years ago, not to say nothin' about no thousand. That's a lotta handsa; I know that much."

"Nobody remembers personally, Admiral," I explained. "But there are written records starting seven thousand years ago in Sumeria, and archeologists have discovered a lot about even earlier times, right back to the beginnings of humanity."

"Whereat is this here 'Smearya'?" she demanded. "Things are good there, you say? Call me 'Betsy.' "

"It's a long way," I admitted. "Sumeria was a country between two rivers. It collapsed thousands of years ago. The same territory now is a poverty-stricken pesthole occupied by fanatical trouble-makers."

"Don't sound no better'n Philly or Jersey," she commented. " 'Seven thousand years'! A body can't hardly get their mind around a number that big. What's it all for, anyways?" She looked around as if noticing the collapsed gas station and the barren fields for the first time.

"That's a question everyone has to decide for himself. The best thinkers we've had have decided it's not just for whatever quick thrills we might get. It has to do with abstract conceptions like ethics and integrity and doing unto others—"

"Yeah, I know that one; 'Do unta others as they'd like to do unta you, on'y do it first.' "

"Not quite, Betsy," I corrected her. "A long time ago, people started noticing they were happier if the people around them were happy, too. The secret is cooperation, instead of dog-eat-dog."

"Yeah, I seen a big Pack once," she reminisced.

"We's out late on a raid over Milford, got cut off, durn nigh, by the scout dogs. Wintertime. We had the sail-sleds, got around, out ahead of em. Ziggy had a fire-gun, shot inta 'em, whole bunch stopped to eat the one he hit. Worked good." She ended on a note of satisfaction.

"People finally discovered there was a better way," I explained. "If everybody looks out for everybody else, you have a lot of people looking out for you, instead of just one."

She looked surprised; at least her mouth was hanging open. "Yeah," she said. "I can see how that could be. But how'd you ever get anybody to do that?"

"You started by doing it yourself," I told her.

"Thank I'm crazy?" she remarked. "I come up to Banger or Snead and said, 'You fellers hongry? Got some eats over here; come and eat 'em.' They'd knock me in the head. Don't nobody like crazies. Don't blame 'em. Don't like crazies myself." She backed a step, keeping her eyes on me. "*You* ain't a crazy, are you?"

"How would I know?" I asked her. "But let's descend from the realms of philosophical abstraction to the immediate: what will this Bunny do if I just walk in on his headquarters?"

"Kill ye," she grunted. "You ain't thinking about doin' that, are ye?"

"Do you care if I get killed?" I asked, genuinely wanting to know.

"Why should I?" she came back without hesitation.

"That's not the question," I pointed out.

"Well, I don't reckon it's no skin off my butt if you want to get yerself kilt," she ruminated aloud.

"Lessen you got a nice stash someplace nobody elst don't know about. Shame to waste it. Tell me about it, feller, 'fore you go to get kilt."

"That's a stirring appeal, Betsy," I said. "But maybe it's a beginning. Suppose we throw in together for a while? You get me into the settlement, and I'll be sure you're the first to know all my valuable secrets."

She replied, "Ha! Soon's anybody sees you, they'll kill you. You're a Strangy," she reminded me. "On'y reason I never kilt ye, you got that far-gun, dunno *why* you ain't kilt *me* till yet."

"I don't kill everybody I see," I pointed out.

"Done a pretty good job on old Walt and Raunch yonder, and Hickey, too."

"Walt and Hickey aren't dead," I told her for the third time. "They're harmless. Why kill them?"

"Cause next time they see you, they'll sure-bob kill you!" she came back wearily. It seemed I was a very slow pupil.

"Do you know a Bud and Marian?" I asked her.

She stared at me. "They them crazies keeps that shelter full o' sprats?" she demanded in a tone of incredulity.

"All I know is the names," I told her. "Are they over there?" I nodded toward the lights.

"Was the last I looked," she admitted. "What you want with them trash?"

"Personal matter," I said. "I have a message for them from someone." I thought of her, with Tobey's hard hand clamped on her arm, hoped that somehow, after all she'd been through, she was all right now. She was a resourceful girl, with plenty of guts. Tobey would have gotten over his temper fit and thought better of his threats.

But Admiral Betsy was still talking. "Can't he'p no spy," she was saying. "Got no use for Bunny, but what happens to spies is something nobody don't want to get inta."

"Forget all that nonsense." I was feeling impatient. "All I want is to meet Bud and Marian, and get some idea of how things are going, out here away from Tobey's palace."

"Things is going bad," she answered me. "Eats is harder to find all the time. And stuff is falling apart—*good* stuff. And them Jersey fellers is gettin' pushier, poking around. Why old Bunny set up the watch on the strip here and all. You see why it don't do fer no Strangy to come snooping around."

"I intend to be very inconspicuous," I reassured her, then realized she didn't know the word. "I don't want anybody to know I'm there," I explained. "Just help me get to Bud and Marian."

She nodded inattentively. "Then you'll show me yer trove, right? Just ours, won't tell Bunny. That's against the rules, o' course, but we'll handle it careful, prolly won't nobody bother us."

"As for food," I wondered. "Don't you do any farming? This is all prime agricultural land here."

"What's that?" she demanded. "Always using them strange words," she carped.

"Farming," I told her," is tilling the soil and planting crops, and tending them until they're ready to be harvested. Then you eat them."

"Eat weeds?" she scoffed. I shook my head. "Fresh fruits and vegetables," I told her, "and there are useful raw materials, and feed for animals."

"Now you figger yer gonna feed animals?" she jeered. "What ones? Dogs is what you see mostly.

They get their own eats; likely to be us, we don't get back pretty soon."

"I'm talking about farm animals," I tried to say patiently. "Cattle, and sheep, pigs, horses."

"I heard o' some o' them," she conceded. "Seen a big old critter once, some fellers trapped it inside a fence. Had horns on it, out to here." she indicated a space of six feet. "Dern nigh kilt one of 'em; stuck that big old horn right in his laig. He bled some; couldn't walk good after that." She sighed. "*Had* to catch it, they said. Damn thing had been chasing 'em ever' time they tried to go shoppin' down the Mall. So you want to catch some o' them monsters and feed 'em; what for?"

"Yes, I suppose the cattle would have reverted somewhat to the original aurochs type," I mused. "Horses would be OK, just like the wild mustangs out west. Pigs you mentioned. I don't know; might be more like the razorbacks, but sheep would be easy; no genes for violence there."

"I ast you what for," Betsy reminded me.

"Sheep, for wool—and meat," I told her. "Pork and beef, meat; horses, draft animals; and chickens and turkeys for food."

"I heard about crazy folks eats dirt," she told me, looking disgusted. "You talking about eating *animals?* Dogs, maybe? That's plumb nasty." She spat.

"There's nothing nasty about a thirty-eight-ounce U.S. Prime porterhouse, cut an inch and a half thick, broiled rare," I told her, and abruptly I was hungry.

She shook her head impatiently. "I don't know nothing about that," she dismissed my remark.

"I'm try'n'a picture taking a bite outa that big monster with them horns."

I shook my head. "First you tame them, then you can breed for size, disposition, and so on. Then you cut it up properly, cut the hindquarter to give you the loin; then it has to be aged; then you broil it, five minutes on each side. Plenty of salt, some good bread and a nice wine to go with it. You'll see," I assured her.

She was shaking her head again. "I don't want to see," she stated. "I'll stick to regular eats."

"And what are those like?" I followed up.

"*You* know," she told me. "You been eatin' good, anybody can see."

"Back there," I nodded toward the palace lights, "everybody eats good."

"You really don't know how to get eats," she said, as if telling herself.

"I can't believe everybody's been living on nothing but canned goods for all these years. They'd all be dead of deficiency disease."

She stood, dusted off her rump. "Let's go," she ordered, and waved me behind her. "Quiet now, mind you." She headed off into the brush. I followed her, aware of the noises made by my feet crushing dry stalks. I couldn't hear Betsy, ten feet ahead. It was easy enough going in the pre-dawn light, if you didn't count the briars and beggarslice, and the increasingly foul odor. We crossed a couple of fields and veered off to the left to come up on the outlying tents and huts that ringed the more solid structure toward the middle—a former high school building, it looked like. I tried and failed to remember what had been here all those mornings I drove past. The putt-putting of the generator was the dominant sound. The chilly breeze brought the stink strongly now. I heard a chicken screech *ar-ar-are-are!* So they did keep a few after all. Voices were wrangling just ahead in a low hut off to the right. Then I heard someone tramping through the weeds with no more finesse than my own clumsy tiptoe. Betsy halted and waved me forward. When I reached her, she put her face to my ear and whispered.

"Jest old Rusty on a nature call. Watch out fer the trenches, you don't wanta fall inta *them*. Better keep low now." I heard another sound, which turned out to be a pig, rooting in the rubbish and the slit-trenches. Just as well if the locals *didn't* eat that.

"Why don't we swing out and go around this?" I asked her, seeing now that we were approaching a projecting ridge thickly clustered with huts.

"Can't," she admitted. "Got to get to the pit yonder."

"What's the pit?" I wanted to know.

"Where I stay at," she grunted. She had halted and was looking around her as if searching for something on the ground. She said, "Hah!" and took a step to her right and dropped to her knees. There was enough early daylight now to see the full ugliness of the squalid encampment, to match the stink of it.

"Get down, dammit!" she hissed, and made pushing-down motions. I crouched and watched her feel over the bare patch of pebbly ground; I jumped when a trapdoor made of planks rose, spilling dust. Betsy immediately thrust her feet into the black opening thus uncovered and turned to me a face tight with strain.

"Foller me," she hissed. "Just don't say nothin' to nobody: I'll have a eye on you. Go to the end o' the tunnel." Then she slid down and eased the door shut. I lifted it, and was met by a wave of hot, smelly air. I had a little difficulty in finding the floor with my feet. There was a dim light from a kerosene lantern along the plank-walled tunnel.

A man unglued himself from the wall and moved out to block me, but Betsy grabbed his arm and said something to him. All I caught was, ". . . with *me*, Knothead. Get out my way!"

He faded back and Betsy came over and grabbed my arm. "You done okay," she said. "Don't say nothing; soon's they hear the funny way you talk, we're in trouble." She went on to the plank door that blocked the passage about twenty feet along. I came up just as she pulled it open and went through.

I followed into a stench that made the preliminary stink seem like perfume. Even Betsy snorted. "Got to get on them fan-pushers," she remarked.

It was a big, irregularly-shaped room with lots of concrete columns; heaps of rags and piles of trash were scattered all across the floor, weakly-lit by more of the kerosene lamps. People—mostly under fifty, they looked—stood, sat, or lay on the rags. They didn't appear to be paying much attention to us. I looked back.

The door we had come through was set in a crudely-hacked opening in a bare, stained concrete wall. It seemed to be a basement. The black bulk of a coal-burning furnace loomed up in the center of the room, at the center of a radiating array of black-painted ductwork. Betsy was forging ahead along a vaguely defined aisle that threaded among the trash bags, where big rats nibbled undisturbed. I followed, glancing over the gaunt, rag-clad people, male and female, all hollow-eyed, haggard, and very dirty. Nobody tried to catch my eye, nobody spoke, nobody cared. Most of them were doing nothing, except perhaps idly picking at fleas; those who *were* busy, rearranging their ragbeds or fiddling with rusty junk, worked alone. There was no evidence of human cooperation. The small stir our arrival caused damped out within twenty feet. Nobody paid any attention when Betsy came up to a metal door and opened it, with considerable difficulty and the screech of unoiled hinges. There was a flight of concrete steps with a rusty handrail, worn bright along the upper surface. She went up and waited on the landing. The people below moved back.

"Skeered o' the Noocler," she explained when I came up.

"Good luck," she went on. "Old Smily ain't around. He ain't skeered; tried to get in once; had to skull him. Now all we got to do, we got to get up to Two and make it down to my place, no sweat. Come on." She didn't wait for my opinion or questions, but went right up to the next landing with a door marked with a large "2." It opened quietly; she held it open and peered in, then waved me through. After I was through and onto a floor littered with curled chips of composition floor tiles she came through and closed and bolted the door. Just as I was about to ask her where we were going, she brushed past me and made a beeline for a door along the wide hall. It slammed open and a man in bulky furs came through it and saw her and snarled. He had a battered face, perhaps a little better-fed than the folks in the cellar, and he looked displeased, until he saw me; then he looked infuriated. Betsy stepped into his path.

He pushed her aside and came over to me with a long, rangy stride.

"This here yer new sucker?" he demanded, over his shoulder. He was gnawing on a cud of something which produced twin streams of brown juice flowing from the corners of his mouth down into a truly filthy grayish beard, matted and stained and full of twigs and leaf-litter or something worse. I saw a large, healthy louse pop out of concealment in the mustache department of the mass of whiskers. His eyes crossed slightly; the movement had attracted his attention. He slapped his own face with a *smack!* that made *my* face hurt. "Damn do-do bugs," he remarked and returned his attention to me. A large hand planted itself against my chest, and slammed me back against the wall. I managed not to fall down.

I was still weak, I realized. He held me there and I watched him double a fist the size of a pineapple and draw his arm back. My gaze went past him to Betsy, who fumbled under her clothes and brought out a well-worn butcher's knife which had been honed away to a slim finger of steel; there was nothing clumsy about the way she came up behind him and plunged it into his back with an upward sweep. His bleary eyes opened wide and he made an ugly noise and blood joined the brown trickle at the left corner of his chapped mouth. Then he arched his back and twisted to try to put a hand on the spot that hurt. He stumbled back, and suddenly a mouthful of blood burst from his gaping jaws; then he uttered a deep groan and fell abruptly, flat on his back, propped awkwardly by the hilt of the knife. Betsy stepped over him.

"You done good," she stated. "Come on." She grabbed my arm and pulled me away. I was looking down at the dead face that had been alive and full of fury only a moment before. Now it was slack and empty. One eye was half open, as if in a knowing wink.

"That's old Ratsy," Betsy told me. "Likes rats. Some say he eats 'em." She made an exaggerated gagging sound. "Now they'll eat *him*," she added as if that were a good one on old Ratsy.

I didn't acknowledge the introduction. "You killed him," I said, "just like that. What was he doing in your place?"

"Prolly robbin' it," she guessed. "Hadda fix him where he couldn't give the alarm. Old Ratsy don't like Strangies near as good as most folks do." She urged me through the open door into a relatively clean and orderly room furnished with an assortment of wooden crates, a broken chair, and a pallet made of rags.

"Not bad, hey?" she said happily. "Don't know how Ratsy got in here, 'less—" She interrupted herself to look thoughtfully at the lone window, where dawn was glowing full blast now, pink clouds in a blue and gold sky, as perfect as if the world didn't lie dead at its feet.

"Looks like he didn't get nothin'," she remarked. "Nothin' to get."

"What about the body outside?" I asked.

"Rats'll eat it by tomorrow," she said indifferently. "Bones and all," she added, "if one o' them crazies don't find him first. Not likely; nobody don't come up here, reason I got this place all to myself."

"Why not?" I asked. "Why don't people come here, I mean," I explained.

"Skeered," she told me, sounding content. "Don't know how old Ratsy got the nerve. Musta got into some crazy-juice. Wonder he never sold it, 'steada drinking it hisself. Wasted, too," she added. She glanced at me. "Him being dead and all, I mean," she clarified.

"Skeered of what?" was my next question.

"The Noocler, o' course." She grunted.

" 'Nuclear'? Nuclear what?"

"Jest the Noocler," she muttered, as if the subject were indelicate.

"Sorry," I said, "I don't know what that means."

"Big old monster, prolly lives back in these here old dark places," she whispered, as if mentioning the source would summon it.

"Why aren't *you* afraid of this bugaboo?" I demanded. She looked nervous now, or as nervous as five-feet-three of muscle and survival skill could look.

"Can't afford to be," she told me, looking a bit more like her usual assured self. "Snuck up here and 'splored some a long time ago. Just a kid then. Seen nothing but the rats." She changed the subject abruptly. "Got to get my sticker back." Then she paused. "Wait'll the rats are done first," she advised herself, and got busy rummaging in an iron-strapped box by the door.

She came up with some unlabeled number six cans, only slightly rusty. "Got to eat. Old Ratsy never knowed about my stash here." I looked over her shoulder. The layer of cans was under a thick layer of rags.

" 'Fraid to poke in them rags," she explained. "Fulla do-do bugs." She slapped at her forearm as if in confirmation, then she banged the cans together. "Little bug-dirt on 'em, don't hurt none." She went to the table to begin her preparations. I wondered if she planned to offer me any, and if I'd accept.

"You had that knife all along." I heard myself thinking aloud. "When we were out there in the dark, you had plenty of chances. Why didn't you knife me?"

She gave me a sort of "tolerant contempt" look. " 'Cause you trusted me," she said. "Nobody never trusted me before. Seen what a helpless feller you are. I kinda like that, not having to watch every move." Then she showed some brown teeth in a smile as cheery as a flasher caught in the Ladies Room.

"I've got an idea," I told her. "Let's be friends. But I guess you don't know what that is."

She shook her head. "Read about it in a book," she stated, almost defiantly. She looked at me as if daring me to call her a liar. She nodded vigorously. "Yes, I can read," she affirmed. "Old Lady taught me, used to be what they call a teacher, right here in the Place." She waggled her head as if to indicate the former school above. "I was jest a sprat. Liked the pitchers in them books; found some about a place they called 'Oz.' Liked them books real good. Like to go there sometime."

"Then we're friends?" I pressed the point. She paused in her efforts to open a can with a worn-out beer-can church key. "Well, I'm durned if I know how to be one," she told me. "You'll hafta tell me if I screw up or anything."

"That's a deal," I said. "Now, as a friend, how about answering a few questions I have about all this."

"No spying, is all," she reminded me. "Whatcha wanna know about?"

"Was the country invaded and occupied?"

She shook her head. "You better ask easier ones," she said. "I don't know what that means."

"Was there a war with Russia? Did we lose?"

"Never hearn tell o' that 'Rusher,'" she said, frowning. "Only war I know about is when Jersey tried to hustle Dee-Cee. Jersey lost; reason he never taken over Philly. That what you mean, stuff like that ever'body knows?"

"Farther back," I corrected her. "Back when Jersey and DC and Philly were just cities in the United States."

She nodded vaguely. "There you go about that Nice Day," she noted in mild reprimand. "Always thought it was just one o' them fairy tales like I done read about."

So she believed in Oz, but not the United States, which was only a legend called "Nice Day."

The cans contained tuna, beans, and tomato soup. She dug a metal bowl out of somewhere, and dumped it all in together. There were two spoons. It tasted *good*.

After dinner, I tried to tell her where I'd been for some ninety years. She laughed at me. "I *like* bein' friends," she told me. "Maybe this is some of that 'fun' you was saying about."

"Where did you get the canned goods?" was my next query.

"Found the storeroom long yonder," she replied absently, with a nod that seemed to indicate the direction in which we'd been going just before we'd met the late Ratsy. "What I was looking for," she confided, "Old Lady said where they had this storeroom, said the school was a designated hardened shelter, whatever that is, stocked with eats and all, so I come looking. Found it, too, 'fore I found my place here. Good eats, right, feller?"

"Why not call me 'Jackson,' " I suggested.

She said, "Sure," and got up and went over to a boxed-in corner and came back with a warped plastic pitcher half full of slightly murky water. "I don't eat dry, neither," she remarked proudly, and poured a vinyl cup half full for me, and one for herself. I sniffed the water and sipped it. It seemed all right, and I was, I suddenly realized, as thirsty as a camel. I drank it; if it killed me, it killed me.

But it was cool and sweet. Clearly, the old high school had been well-equipped for emergencies; probably drawing water from a deep well with a back-up DC pump.

"Folks'd kill fer this here," she remarked, sipping her *Chateau La Pompe*. She was scrupulous about wiping the plates and putting the empties in a plastic bag of which she seemed to have an abundant supply.

"Burn it later on," she explained. "None o' them kookie-bugs around here."

"I don't suppose there's a stash of old magazines and newspapers around anywhere," I said.

I was surprised when she nodded. "Know what them is," she stated a bit proudly. "Old Lady used to tell me about the olden days, showed me the pitchers and all in them newspapers. She wasn't right in the head." Betsy tapped her own hard-looking gourd. "Said about how folks used to walk around in broad daylight, go in the stashes and trade paper fer eats and good shoes and everything. She was one good old lady, though. Couldn't remember it clear though, she said. Read about it. Then there was the Strikes."

"Tell me more," I urged. "What strikes?"

"Well," she got out some fingers to count on, "there was the bank strike, and the tax strike; that was the big one, she said; and the big money-burn, that ain't quite the same, and the law strike—don't know what all them thangs was—and seems like there was some more I useta know: the hospital strike, that's one, and the big energy strike, and—wait a minute, Jackson, I'll show ya the book place. I bet you can read, right? Come on. Won't be no scroungers around now. Keepers time."

"What are Keepers?" was my next naive query. She only grinned, didn't tell me "everybody knows that," and said, "Bunny's head-hitters is what they are. Don't nobody stir when them mothers is makin' the rounds."

"Do they come up here?" I asked. She shook her head. "Tole you, they're all scairt o' the Noocler. All 'cept me—and I guess you, too, Stran——Jackson." She got to her feet. "Come on," she urged. "Not far." She eased the door open and peeked out. I caught a glimpse of a boiling heap of gray-brown rats covering the departed Ratsy: a fitting end for one of his name. She skirted him and started along the corridor, not looking back to see if I was following. I was, past a wide cross-corridor with more of the cryptic signs, reading AM-AB-7-13 and ST ONE, ph 03L. She went right past it; the light was dimmer here, but still good enough to see the rat bones littering the floor, the odds and ends of broken glass and plastic and metal that the last ones out had dropped when the "evacuate" order came down.

Betsy stopped at a door like all the other doors, shooed off a cat-sized rat, and opened the door. Inside I could see sagging shelves heaped with dusty bales of old paper, more bales on the floor, and some loose copies, plus dust, dust, dust. I went past these and picked up a loose paper. It was in traditional newspaper format, but the "paper" was a smooth-textured synthetic. I shook off the powdery dust, amid which were a few flakes with print on them. Newsprint hadn't held up, but the switch to a more permanent version had come in time to preserve the record—I hoped.

The one I held was the *Jasperton Gazette Times–Courier* and the date, February 18, 2013. The lead story was headed, DISTRIBUTION CENTER TO CLOSE, and the first few lines were devoted to assurances that the story was approved at all levels of de facto government. Honest. Seemed the easy life was over. All supervision of goods-distribution at the Central and outlying points was discontinued as of Friday. OK; whatever had happened, governmental control hadn't survived it.

I picked through the loose issues of the *Courier*; the earliest date I found was 2008. I caught glimpses of headlines, found one about the tax strike Betsy had mentioned. I read a few paragraphs before I got lost in obscure references to what must have been vigilante organizations and "temporary measures."

It seemed the patient citizens of what Betsy called "Nice Day" had finally gotten sick of working hard so they could pay for foreign and domestic giveaways, and had just stopped paying. They couldn't lock up three hundred million people, so the government—at all levels—had tried to wing it by printing paper money. That hadn't worked; it ended in 2009 with the big money burn. There were photos of haystack-sized heaps of currency blazing, while eager citizens threw on more.

After that was the military strike, when the boys in uniform all decided to go home and to hell with it. Nobody bothered to vote in the elections of 2012. As the factories and distribution systems broke down, the mines and other sources of raw materials closed up, and the food shortage generated masses of people who, it seemed, were astonished that the old familiar Piggly Wiggly store no longer carried all their favorite brands. Burning the stores didn't help.

The last remnants of the Army were detailed to loot the stores and stockpile the non-perishable foods, while work was expedited on means of preserving meat, dried beans, dairy products, eggs, and cereals. They succeeded in time to treat and store considerable stocks of basics. That was the last organized effort and apparently it had been a heroic one, if there were still "eats" to be scrounged even now.

After that just about everything collapsed. Mob-rule was overthrown by mob-leader rule. The "barons" fought it out among themselves. Society, it seemed, had reverted to a pre-medieval state, with the feudal system reinvented. All this was between the lines, which consisted of hastily impro-vised jargon about "patriotic volunteers" and "popular mass action." Finally, Mallon had stepped in to claim his share. There was no foreign news, except a few oblique references to the May Revo-lution, in Russia, and a hasty formation of the long-discussed Western European Union, plus one in South America, both of which soon folded. Asia reverted to isolationism, after destroying Japan, which had attempted to "restore order."

Betsy sat patiently and waited, occasionally ask-ing me what I was doing. We both sneezed a lot, and after a while I got tired of my research. What, after all, did it matter? It had happened—not the dreaded nuclear war, fear of which still haunted the ruins of collapsed buildings and underground installations—but internal collapse, as people just stopped following the rules. It had taken humanity fifty thousand years to evolve those rules, but only a few decades to destroy them, and the culture they had produced. Even in my day the attack on "the Establishment" had begun by people who must have been astounded when, suddenly, there *was* no Establishemnt—and no electric service, no phones, no water distribution, and—unthinkably —no telly. It hadn't occurred to them that hassling and then destroying the "pseudo-intellectuals" would have any such results. Their idea of going back to nature was to drive the air-conditioned camper to the park and live off canned peaches. They were like kids who would define "food" as "stuff ma puts on the table and makes you eat." A car was "the thing that sits in the driveway and your old man doesn't want to give ya the keys to." "Where do cars come from?" would get you, "You get em at the car place."

Now they were finding out the hard way that light isn't just something you get when you flip the switch, and water wasn't just what comes out when you turn the tap, and even telly didn't necessarily happen when you turned the knob. There had been great indignation, which had been expressed by hunting down and hanging the former managers, executives, financiers, and anyone who wasn't a union man. By the year 2060, I estimated, society had hit bottom and what was left of the population was firmly, though chaotically, under the heels of the barons.

26

The following day Betsy led me out cautiously into the former stadium which had become a sort of market-*cum*-forum where all the activity went on. "Well, you're gonna hafta learn how to handle yourself sometime," were her parting words.

I soon lost sight of Betsy in the crowd, and within a minute five tall men in black-dyed clothes hemmed me in silently and jabbed something hard into my spine. They conducted me to a former office in the field house where an immensely fat man with a bald kewpie-head with odd, pointy ears sat, or lolled, on an upholstered recliner loaded with cushions.

He waved a cigarette holder at me and said, "What's this?" in a high, squeaky voice. "Where did you find him, General?"

The Blackie thus addressed stepped forward, gave a Hollywood, or shade-the-eyes salute and said,

"Come out the Old Place with Admiral Betsy, sir."

"Overpowered the Admiral, eh?" Bunny—it had to be him—squeaked.

"Nossir; she was *with* the Strangy," someone volunteered.

"Prolly her prisoner," Bunny squeaked. "Bring her in." He snapped his fingers and dismissed the man with a glance; he turned and looked expectantly at the door. General muttered to one of his party, who hurried away, and came back half an hour later with a furious Betsy.

Once hauled to her feet in front of Bunny's desk she spat. "I got to report these here scummies o' yours laid hands on me, Bunny," she screeched, as if he hadn't seen them haul her into his presence.

"Had to, Bett," he piped mildly. "You was aiding this here Strangy, come to kill me."

"He never done no sich of a thang!" she came back, shooting me a glance. Her dialect seemed to have reverted to the bucolic. "Try to use what little brains you got!" she yelled. "This here feller is from the Baron hisself! Got a hot personal message for ya!"

Bunny shifted a little in his big chair. "Hold on, Bett—" He was cut off by another yell from Betsy.

"Don't 'Bett' me, you, Bunny! That's 'Admiral,' I'll thank ya to remember!"

He held up a pudgy hand, "All right, all right," he squeaked. "Git yer hands offin the Admiral," he ordered the two gorillas who were holding her down. They complied and stepped back, not looking at each other, or at the General, who started to puff himself up for a blast, but thought better of it.

"Now, Admiral," Bunny squeaked. "What's this about a message from his Grace yonder? Heard a lotta activity from the palace last few days: shots fired, vehicles on the move. Figgered he had a little revolution on his hands."

"You figgered wrong!" Betsy snarled. "Got the Great Troll broke loose from the 'chantment is what he done! Got big new plans, and you was lucky he was gonna give you a 'portant job of work to do! Sent this here feller to tell you all about it. Could be now he might not wanta, you treating him—and me—the way you done!" She pulled her five feet of muscle and fury into a defiant pose. "Coulda been a Big Man," she muttered. "Coulda got outa this here hog-pen."

"I done nothing, Bett!" Bunny expostulated. "All I done was—"

"Ye'r the Man here!" Betsy yelled back at him. "Ye'r responsible! But maybe it ain't too late," she added, and looked at me.

"Sure it ain't too late," Bunny agreed eagerly. He sat up in his chair and tried to look business-like. He gave me a look that might have been apologetic, or maybe his dinner hadn't agreed with him.

"Get this straighten' out," he squeaked, then looked at the General and tilted his head. "Get out," he ordered, and they cleared the room. I went over and sat in one of the chairs.

"How I 'pose to *know?*" Bunny whined. "Got standing orders stop anybody going in or out. You know that." He looked accusingly at Betsy. "Why I sent you and Hickey out there," he grumbled. "On the job, that's my style." He looked at me with a slight return of defiance. "What's the message?"

"You're to mobilize your full strength and report to His Grace by sunup one week from tomorrow," I improvised. Betsy looked surprised, but covered it with a sneeze. She wiped her nose on her sleeve and said. "See, Bunny, he's countin' on ya!"

Bunny—no title for him, he was the Man—patted his paunch and squeaked. "I done homage fer one hundred and fifty—that's six handsa," he said in an aside as if explaining to himself. "Reckon I can't muster more'n five handsa; had the dirt-sickness and all that. Do my best." He gave me a calculating look.

"Well, His Grace *did* give me a little discretion," I conceded. "Five handsa it is."

"Reckon you and the Admiral could do with a hot bathe-off and some good eats," he suggested. Before I could agree, Betsy spoke up: "No time fer none o' that," she rapped. "Got to see to my regiment first-off." She started toward the door, then remarked over her shoulder, "You can come with me, feller; find a spot for you in the reserve guard."

Just like that we walked out, gave the General and his boys a glance as we went past, and were back out in the sunshine, where groups of people were standing around, or wandering aimlessly. A few fistfights were in progress, but nobody paid any attention.

"Tricky games yer playin', feller," she told me when there was no one within ten feet.

"You didn't give me much to go on."

"You done all right," she conceded. "Place'll be a crazy-pen. Why'd you give the sucker a full week?"

"I need time to figure the next move."

She nodded. "Good idear. Now let's go to my place and get the boys moving. I got the Regiment o' Guards," she added. " 'Sponsible fer the personal safety of the Man."

"That's convenient," I commented. "How big is this outfit of yours?"

"Got about four handsa," she said contentedly. "Since Horny up and died, got his bunch."

I trailed along while she made her way through the noisy, ragged, dirty, sullen-looking crowd scattered all across the former playing-field. She picked out a man or woman here and there and spoke to them in a low voice. One tall redheaded fellow said something, turning away, and she threw him on his back with one swift motion. In half an hour, she had a ragged column of fours trailing us. Then she halted and made a short and to-the-point speech and finished, "Now, scat!" and they dispersed in all directions.

"Can we find Bud and Marian now?" I asked her with all due respect. She nodded and started off through a door under the stadium. It was dark and evil-smelling, and shadowy figures lounged against the walls. She stopped once and snapped:

"You! Tench! You got four handsa to fall in. We got a job of work to do!" She moved on without waiting to see his reaction. "Got to make sure they got ever'thang they need, 'fore we have to march," she explained, and nodded to herself.

Where the passage emerged into the bright day on the parking-lot side, there was a structure of sorts, built against the wall, partly covering a nine-foot high A-frame. It was made of odd-sized pieces of canvas and plastic, patched but still full of holes, all propped up with sticks like a parody of a circus big top. A chain was stretched around the periphery.

Back of the chain, a boy of about ten was
crouched behind a heap of rotted boards. He rose
and, with an intent expression on his unwashed
face, pegged a piece of rusty metal at a plump
woman with two bleary-faced kids in tow. He
missed, but she stopped to curse him in terms that
would have made me blush if I'd known how.
Betsy kept a keen eye on the marksman; when he
looked her way, his gaze fell, and he turned and
disappeared among the sagging tarps.

The plump woman went through a gap in the
chain, dragging the now-squalling brats behind
her, lifted a flap, and disappeared somewhere inside the tent.

"Marian there," Betsy said. "I give her the sign;
old Bud'll be here directly." Marian wasn't quite
the gracious lady Renada had so lovingly described.
No doubt time and wishful thinking had distorted
her childhood recollections, unless Marian had gone
downhill fast. I waited and tried to analyze the
incredibly rich and varied stench from the shelter.

Bud was a tall, incredibly skinny fellow of perhaps fifty, with no hair except some discouraged-
looking gray muttonchops with food particles, and
a beard to match. His mouth was working as he
came into view:

"Got no time to waste on no damn foolishness,"
he was complaining in a high, reedy voice. He
came over to the chain and gave Betsy a puzzled
look. "What you want with me, Admiral-woman?"
he inquired in a tone that said that whatever it
was, she'd come to the wrong place.

Betsy nodded her head toward me and said

nothing. I knew a cue when I saw one; I cleared my throat and said, "Renada sends her best wishes."

He staggered back as if I'd hit him in the face with a flounder. "Don't know no Renada," he bitched. "Got work to do. You run along, Strangy. You'll get no sport here." As he completed his speech, which sounded as though he'd memorized it, the plump woman popped out of another flap and fetched up beside him.

"What about Rennie, a sweet child?" she demanded. "Ought to be well-growed by this time. Be a beauty, too. Nice teeth, even." She showed her own blackened stumps, as if for contrast.

"Give her all the best, special-like," she bragged and paused as if awaiting an argument, then added. "Need stuff here, eats, other stuff. Get you a couple fine boys and a gal. Two handsa prime cans fer each one." I had a feeling she'd ad-libbed those last three words.

I shook my head. "Forget it, Marian," I suggested. "Don't need any snot-noses right now. Need men."

"And good, tough gals," Betsy added. "And got no eats—all fer the Man's personal service, o' course, and hurry up."

Marian started to snuffle. "Had to give up little Herby and Snot and Billy, too," she whimpered. "Like my own babies, bless 'em, gone these two handsa winters. Can't see how we'll do without 'em."

"Okay, a handa the good stuff," Betsy conceded. "Fer the lot."

Marian looked at me with a satisfied expression on her muddy face. "What's that about Renada?

My special pet, that one was." She seemed to be talking more to herself than to me. "Kept her clean," she added. "A virgin—not even her brothers —and taught her fancy habits. No nose-pickin', warshin' off a lot, too, di'n't even have to whup her to it. Nice build on her now, I bet."

"You did a good job, Marian," I told her. "She sends you her best wishes."

She spat, missing my shoe. "Can't eat no wishes. Ole Bairn oughta be ashamed—"

Bud's backhand caught her across the mouth. "Woman's upset," he explained. "Had a couple of the new ones die on her last night, after she put time in on 'em, too. Damn shame." He wiped his mouth with the all-purpose back of his bony hand. "Wanna see inside?" he inquired doubtfully, and led the way along a crooked path alongside the tent and under a pinned-back flap into a profound stench of human waste and decay. It was a dark, malodorous cavern where, under the low, sagging ceiling, I could barely make out in the dim light rows of filthy pallets, about half of them occupied by disheveled children, either lying, curled up, or sitting, all ages from undiapered infants to stringy teenagers wearing diapers; both sexes, some of whom were vigorously copulating, hetero- or homosexually about equally.

"Like you can see," Bud told me, "they're all fed, clothed, and housed in outa the weather."

Or the worst of it, I reflected. It was clammy and drafty, and no doubt when it rained, it leaked plenty. After all, handsome old Bud couldn't be expected to fix *all* the leaks.

"Need he'p here," Bud added.

"What do they eat?" I asked.

"Same as us," he said proudly, coming up beside me, with Betsy. "Prime stuff. Got our own stash. Nothing fancy—turned that in to the Man, o' course—but good solid eats. You don't see none of 'em starvin', do you?"

I didn't, but it was hard to imagine Renada coming from this. "How'd she get in the garbage cans?" I asked. Bud made an elaborate shrugging gesture. "Hadda hide her," he explained. "Troops'da took her. Getting purty, even then. Worked okay, too, if she wouldn't of sneezed."

"See you got yer eye on that little gal yonder," Marian commented, to me. "You can pick 'em. Call Jeannie. Good worker, and she'll fill out good soon now. Had her two handsa. Let her go fer half yer stash."

I declined, to her surprise, even when she lowered the price to one case o' the good stuff.

"So much for altruism," I said to Betsy. "This pair are running a slave-market."

Betsy nodded. "Welcome to it," she dismissed the matter. The girl I'd been accused of watching, one of the older ones, was a nice—for this place—looking kid of about eighteen, with red hair that was almost combed. She was carrying a messy baby on her hip, and bending over another kid lying on his rags, crying.

"You be quiet now, Runny," she was saying to the boy, about eight, I guessed—a little older than Timmy had been. For a moment I tried to imagine my little guy here in this hellhole, but I quickly changed the subject.

"I'll find you some eats," Jeannie was saying

comfortingly to the whimpering boy. "You jest take a nap now, Runny, and I'll see Joey don't bother you none."

As she straightened up, a bigger kid with a pimply face already twisted in a cynical grin sauntered over and said, "Lissen, Jeannie, I got a big old squirrel I'll swap ye fer one o' them cans. Okay?" He managed to kick a clod of the plentiful dirt onto Runny's pallet, then knelt in mock solicitude and started rummaging. He eased a whittled wooden knife out from under the rag bed and into his pocket. Jeannie told him to put it back. He rolled sideways, toward me, got to his feet and started to run. I put out a foot and tripped him. Jeannie gave me a grateful look, and recovered the toy and gave it back to Runny.

"Made it hisself," she told me as if explaining why she hadn't permitted the kid to be robbed. "Pore kid ain't got much," she added. Joey was back on his feet, with tears making mud of the dirt on his face.

"Why not whittle one of your own?" I asked the little thief.

"Got no knife nor nothin'," he blurted.

"Okay, lay off the smaller kids and I'll get you one," I said. He looked startled and looked around as if searching for the hitch, before he ran off.

"That was nice, Mister," Jeannie said softly. "But pleasser, git it fer him like you said. Hate to see a kid disappointed, even that Joey."

"Dont' worry, Jeannie," I reassured her. "I won't forget. And speaking of 'nice,' where'd you learn that word? You're the only nice thing I've seen here. What are you doing in the midst of this mob of murderous yahoos?"

"Paw raised me," she told me, her head erect and pride in her eye. "My paw was big Frank Julius Day, grandson o' Mander Day hisself. Paw was kilt here last year. Nobody never messed with him, nor me, neither. I know I'm sort of strange, but I ain't crazy. I jest *like* to help folks, specially the young ones."

"Maybe there's hope for the human race yet."

"I never heard o' that race. That one against Jersey, or what?"

"It means 'people,' " I explained. "All people are part of the human race."

She said "oh," doubtfully, and was turning away to intercept a little girl of about three who was darting among the forest of adult legs and crying. As she did, a big burly fellow in threadbare dogskin knocked her aside and made a grab for the child. I caught her and noticed how thin she was under her layers of salvaged clothing. The big fellow halted and turned back to give me an unfriendly look from red-rimmed eyes. I could smell gin from a yard away.

He took an open-handed swing at Jeannie which missed because I pulled her back. I took a careful grip on his outstretched arm and bent the elbow backward far enough to bring him to his knees, yowling. A circle had already formed; Jeannie, holding the three-year-old, was crowded into the second rank. I let go the arm and Big Boy started up; I gave him the side of my foot under his chin, and he back-flipped and lay still. People were already turning away. What was one more fight?

As soon as he got to all fours, I kicked him in the rump hard enough to put his cheek back in the dirt. Betsy tugged at my arm. "Leave him be, Jackson," she said in my ear.

"Kill him," somebody suggested, and the spectator closest to him kicked him in the ribs and jumped back. I pushed a couple of eager volunteers back and knocked a fellow away from Jeannie as he was pushing her aside to take her spot. While I was distracted, the crowd closed behind me and I heard them kicking Big Boy to death. He made a horrible gargling sound and collapsed facedown in the dirt. I pulled Jeannie over beside me and asked her, "Where can we go to get clear of this?"

She pulled away slightly to look me in the face. "Ain't no place, Mister," she said. "The whole world is the same, all the way to far as you can see. You know that, good's me."

"Let's try, anyway," I suggested and put an arm across her shoulders and began to bull my way through the crowd jostling for a look at the fresh corpse. One fellow thrust his whiskers, and a case of terminal halitosis, into my face. "Yer the one kilt him?" he demanded. "Good work, Strangy. Terrible mean feller. Likes to stomp the small ones. Kilt one a little bigger'n that 'n"—he meant the tot Jeannie was carrying—"here jest a whicken ago, over the platform."

"Not me," I told him. "I just dropped by on my way to Ashtabula." He disappeared.

Jeannie tugged at my sleeve. "Whereat's that? Purty clothes you got, feller. You from that there Ash-what-you-said?"

"Never heard of it, Jeannie," I assured her. "I'm from here, but not now, if you know what I mean."

"I don't," she said. "You're a strange kinda feller," she went on uncertainly. "Even fer a Strangy."

"It's a long story. I'll tell you sometime."

"You look dead tard," she told me, squinting up at me. "I can smell it, too, a feller gets too tard. You got to lay down. Come on."

She tugged and prodded me through the press to one of the former gates and urged me to sit down in the shelter of the retaining wall under the bleachers. I sat half way and fell the rest. She made a distressed sound and told me to go to sleep. I must have slept, because I was aware of awakening, with someone shaking me. I tried to stay asleep, but it didn't work. I considered carefully and reached the momentous decision to open my eyes. That was a mistake; they were twin pits of burning fire. I started to rub them, but somebody grabbed my hands, and Jeannie's voice said, "You jest hold still now, Mister." It was easy to obey her. Soooo easy . . . something cool touched my hot eyes and ran down.

I was waking up again. Why "again?" I wondered, then remembered my eyes. They were still closed and felt easy now. No itch. Better keep them closed. Someone tugged at my arm and I went along.

"Got to get formed up fer drill now, Boy," Betsy said. "Old Bunny's out and his special boys are cracking heads. Come on."

I stumbled and reflexively opened my eyes; they worked, blearily, but were clogged with something gooey. I wiped at my left eye and looked at my fingers: half-dried blood.

"Skunk hit ye from behind," Betsy told me. "Gal here put some stuff on; ain't bleeding no more. I got to go.

"You report in, now, boy," she added in farewell, "or it'll be ya ass—and mine, too."

I felt in my pockets, found the GI field kit I'd put there a thousand years ago, in another life, and got out the issue tissue. I wiped my eyes, which felt OK now, and could see again. Jeannie was close beside me, still carrying the kid, looking up at me with big brown eyes that were much too innocent for this world.

I saw Big Boy loom up behind her, bloody but still alive after all. One tough sonofabitch. He had a sort of pleased look on his battered face. He veered off to the left, and I thought he was going to go around, but instead, when he got beside Jeannie, he set himself and hit her with a full roundhouse swing of a fist that looked barely smaller than a peanut-fed ham.

The blow knocked her ten feet, and the squalling infant rolled another yard, to be kicked away by a six-year old into whose nest she had blundered. Big Boy gave me a dirty look and half-turned away.

I'd have to see him later. I went to Jeannie and she twisted onto her back and I saw her face, what was left of it. She was breathing raggedly and trying to expel blood from her mouth. I lifted her to a sitting position and helped her get it clear. Her nose was flat and a broken tooth showed through her split lip. One eye didn't look quite right; it had been knocked half out of its socket and the lower eyelid was beneath the eyeball. She was trying to say something.

"See to Teentsy," she managed. I eased her back down and went over to the baby. The baby was dead, lying like a rag doll, as pale as wax; her neck was broken, her head at an obtuse angle against her shoulder.

"Aw, Teentsy," a small boy nearby said, and went over and knelt and took her small, doll-like hand. A hard-faced woman came up and snatched him away. I went back to Jeannie, and fended off a number of people who seemed disinclined to step over her. I had to grab one fellow's leg and dump him as he was about to plant his bare foot on her chest. When I glanced at Jeannie, for a moment I thought she was dead, too. Then blood bubbled from her smashed nose; she was breathing. I scooped her up and saw Marian dithering over a clump of curious but not excited kids. I asked where I could take Jeannie.

"Leave her be," she snarled.

"She'll be trampled to death."

"Ain't no hide offen *my* rump."

I took the badly injured girl over to a heap of rags by the tent-wall and got her as comfortable as I could. She moaned and rolled her head. Blood in her hair was clotting and sticking to things. A boy of ten was standing by, gaping at her.

"She daid, Strangy?" he asked me, not as if it mattered much.

I told him "not yet," and said, "I don't suppose you have a doctor around here?"

The kid dug in a toe and looked at me sideways. "What's that?" he wanted to know.

I tried to explain that it was a person who made a fat living from other people's suffering, and he nodded vigorously. "You mean ole Medic," he told me.

"Can you bring him?" I asked, and handed him a piece of the hard chocolate bar from my field kit. He took it, sniffed it, nibbled, grinned a toothless grin, and said, "Sure, Strangy," and backed away.

Half an hour later a small, wiry fellow wearing a brown-crusted butcher's apron came over. "Boy said you had some trade goods," he grumped and glanced at Jeannie.

"What the hell you do to her?" he demanded, and went to one knee beside her, and shook his head. "What they call the concussion," he announced. "She's took bad."

"Can you clear her nose so she can breathe?" I asked him. He gave me a startled look. He had a weasel-like face, complete with little sharp teeth. Absently, he took the pulse in her left breast.

"Not a bad-looking kid, I bet," he commented. "Was, anyway. That nose ain't never going to look like nothing again. Here, you hold this." He handed me a flat case in well-worn black leather.

I followed instructions, and at the same time discouraged a fat woman who seemed intent on lying down on Jeannie's pallet, as if it were unoccupied.

"Git, you, Sally," Medic said. He snapped open the case and took out an only slightly rusty set of tongs, and began to probe in the flattened nose, releasing more blood. He brought out an ivory white bone chip, and then another.

"Breathe good, now," he predicted. From somewhere under his raggy trenchcoat he fetched a wooden box containing dirty gauze strips, began packing it in her nostrils, and the bleeding slowed to a stop.

"Keep her down and maybe tomorrow I can feed her some. That'll be two handsa prime tin, Strangy. Kid said you had some fancy, too."

I told him I'd pay him as soon as I collected the stuff—

"You *got* a nice stash, ain't you?" he interrupted. "Kid said about the fancy. I'll take some o' that, now."

I broke off another piece of hard chocolate and he grabbed it and popped it into a mouth like an unhealed wound.

"Moy oh moy," he mumbled, drooling brown juice. "Gimme the rest." He got to his feet and held out a hard-looking hand. I told him to be back every hour until further notice, if he wanted all that fancy, and returned my attention to Jeannie. At least the medical profession hadn't changed much.

27

By the next morning, Jeannie was breathing all right, so I went for a walk, a sort of scouting expedition away from the school grounds. The density of huts gradually decreased until I was clear of all but the smell. There was a stretch of secondary road that had once been paved. I hoppped from one patch of blacktop to another, like fording a river on broken ice-slabs.

About half a mile to the east I saw a small masonry house, perched all alone on a hillside; probably the residence of whoever had once worked the former farm I was crossing. It looked almost intact until I saw the boarded-over holes in the roof, and the scaled and mildewed paint, plus some woodwork that was falling apart. A thin trickle of smoke was coming from one of the two chimneys. The weeds were even hacked off short where the front lawn used to be. There was a small kitchen-garden, and a couple of tough-looking chickens pecked listlessly in a pen in one corner. The garage had collapsed on a low, wide car, a long time ago.

As I came up, a man came out to look me over. He was early-middle-aged and looked lean and fit, but his face, shaven for a change, was lined and tired-looking. I headed over toward him and arranged a smile on my face. When I got within hailing distance I said, "Nice place you have here."

"We're doing our best," he replied. "Anybody could do the same."

"Sure," I agreed, "but that might involve a little work. They're too smart for that."

He grinned, not as if it was something he was accustomed to. "Come on in," he said. He advanced and offered a hand to be shaken. "Name's Jackson," he told me.

"Coincidence," I told him. "So's mine." I wondered how he happened to know his ancestral name. Not many I'd met did.

"Come inside and meet the w-woman," he suggested. I had the feeling he'd almost said "wife." I came up the cracked-and-patched-with-pebbles walk and accompanied him up to the front door. The stumps of two immense old junipers flanked it. He noticed my glance.

"*Had* to cut 'em," he said, almost apologetically. "Got to leaning on the house. Feared the next wind might bring 'em down on the roof. Roof's the hardest," he confided. "I got patches on the patches."

I noticed there was glass in some of the windows, and it was even clean. Other panes were broken out and boarded over or stuffed with rags.

He opened the door and waved me in. I was amazed. It looked like a living room, with nearly intact furniture and no impromptu fireplace on the carpet, which was worn to the backing, but clean-swept. I looked around; no dust-clogged spider-webs, no layer of dirt over everything.

"You keep it real nice," I said. He nodded. "Janey," he explained. "She loves to look at the pitchers in the old books like *Ladies Housekeeping* and that, and then we go to the Mall and hunt us up some stuff looks like the pitchers. Takes a lot of warshing and that, but she's a tough little gal, rather work than set in a mess, she says. I he'p when I can," he admitted modestly. He pointed to the pails placed around the room. "Move 'em ever' time it takes to raining. My job to keep the bugs and critters out, too. We found some stuff over the Mall fer that. Janey can read good, seen on the cans where you can keep bugs out thataway."

He interrupted himself to call for Janey, and she answered and came in through a dining room, complete with table and chairs and sideboard, tucking up her hair, which was actually combed. She was a nice-looking lady of maybe thirty, wearing a clean shirt and skirt, and with no visible dirt on her face. Suddenly I was acutely aware of my own unwashed condition, my filthy coverall, scuffed boots, and dirty fingernails.

"Found a cousin," Jackson told her. "Name's Jackson, same as ours." He looked at me. "Where you from, cousin? What's yer first name? Mine's Harv."

"Torrance," I told him.

He looked startled. "Now I *know* we're kin," he said. He sounded pleased. "Had a ancestor name 'Torrance.' I guess yer prob'ly kin to old Ban Jackson, over Jersey."

I shook my head. "I don't know him."

"He *looks* like a Jackson," Janey said approvingly and came up to me and looked me in the face.

"Reckon you can find yer cousin some nice clothes, Harv," she told him. "Prolly like to warsh off, too, wouldn't you, feller?"

I admitted I would. At that moment, something came sailing in through an open window-frame and impacted on the carpet in a spatter of mud. Nothing exploded. Harv and Janey just stood there, but I went flat against the wall and risked a quick look out. A ragged bunch of teenaged and younger kids, male and female, were busy prying stones from the driveway. I looked at Harv. He was patting Janey's shoulder; she looked mad.

"Shouldn't we run them off?" I asked. Harv shook his head. Janey went back into the kitchen.

"Them ain't the baduns," Harv told me. Janey came back with a dustpan and broom and started on the mess.

"They're bad enough," I suggested. Harv shook his head. "Baduns throw through the glass," he explained. "And throw fire on the roof. These here sprats just got nothing to do. Even run the baduns off, one time. Wisht I could talk to 'em," he added wistfully. "Make somethin' of em."

The gang went directly to the garden and began pulling up plants; a potato came through the same broken window, followed by a carrot.

"Dirt-eater," the hoodlums were shouting now. "Dirt-eater!" Then one reached into the chicken-pen and grabbed a startled bird by the neck; he mimed taking a bite from one wing and threw the fowl back inside the cage. The chant got louder.

"Why do you put up with this?" I wanted to know. Harv picked up the two vegetables from the rug, looked them over critically. "Look good," he commented and handed them over to Janey. She sobbed.

"Nothin short o' killing them sprats do any good," Harv said. "Don't hold with too much killin'."

"But your food—"

"We got enough," Harv interrupted, as if it was an old story, told too often. "They never spoil it all."

I felt impatient with him. This was no time or place for saintliness.

Harv went to the door. He opened it, ducked as another spud missed him, and stepped outside.

"You, Pokey," he called, "and Red, you, too! Come in here, I need to talk to ye!" He stepped back inside under a barrage of stones and pieces of carrot, but through the window I saw two of the younger boys take a few steps toward the door before the taunts of the others turned them back.

"Them two come up once," Harv told me. "Wanta talk. Others won't let 'em. Could straighten them boys out."

Well, the idea did him credit, but he had about as much chance of taming these yahoos as he did of coaxing a pup out of a wolf-pack to be a pet pooch. I was still looking out at the yelling gang. A redheaded kid of about ten—one of the two boys who had almost responded to Harv's appeal—came up behind a bigger kid who was chopping the tops off the potato plants and, choosing his spot, hit him a pretty good lick behind the ear with a stick. The bigger kid stopped what he was doing, looked around, spotted Red, and started toward him, but Pokey, who hadn't noticed the byplay, happened to stick out a foot that the big kid tripped over. He helped him up, helped brush the mud off his fur pants. Maybe Harv had something going after all.

Janey showed me the bathroom and gave me a bucket of hot water and a lump of pink soap, some strange towels made of an absorbent synthetic, and a clean shirt. I took a whore-bath and came out feeling more human.

"Would ye like to take some soup, cousin?" Janey asked me. "Got egg and taters in it," she added apologetically. "Might not want it."

"I'd love it, Janey," I said fervently. Harv and I followed her into the kitchen, which was a small, cluttered space with a table made of a door, and a brick fireplace built on the permoleum floor. The soup smelled good. I took the stool Harv offered me, Janey put a full bowl in front of me, and I dipped in. It needed salt, but tasted marvelous.

"Call us 'dirt-eater,' " Harv commented. "Better'n prime stuff. Anyway, got no prime."

"I grew up on farm-grown food," I told them.

"Where was that at?" they both asked at the same time.

"Not far from here, in one way," I said. "A long way in another."

"You mean yonder in that Philly place?" Janey asked, not as if she believed it.

"What about the Noocler?" Harv added.

"That's just a legend," I told them. "There's no such thing anymore." I hoped I was right.

"What's that 'lejin'?" he asked me. Janey nodded, her eyes on me.

"An old story that may have once had some basis in truth," I defined. "But usually embroidered with the supernatural, and local traditions."

"You talk strange, Cousin," Harv told me. "Lotsa big words I never heard folks say before."

I nodded. "Bad habit of mine. Comes from reading too many books."

Janey nodded back. "*We* can read," she told me modestly.

"Can read good," Harv confirmed, nodding in turn toward his wife. "Janey 'specially."

"Where'd you learn?" I wanted to know.

"Lady name of Woman taught us," Harv said, almost reverently. "Wonderful lady. Used to he'p us sprats. That's how come I met Janey. She died here a while back, Woman did. Just got too old, I reckon." He added proudly, "We taken good care of her. She had some funny ways, but she taught us about warshing off, and stuff like that. Showed Janey how to cook up these fine eats."

"I've heard of Woman," I told Harv. "A lady named Renada told me about her."

"Wondered whatever happen to little Rennie," Janey said. "Purty little gal. Disappeared one day. Long time ago."

"She's all right," I reassured her. "The Baron had her, but she's fine now."

They agreed that was good, though they'd never heard of the Baron letting his slaves go free.

"I helped her a little," I admitted.

They both looked at me and said, "Why?"

"She helped me," I said. "Beside which, she's a pretty gal—and nobody should be anybody's slave."

What Janey put on the table next was an omelette with a few vegetables and some diced chicken. I never ate anything better in my life. Janey noticed my enthusiasm.

"Better not tell you what's in that, Cousin," she said. "Might think it's too nasty. Took me a long time 'fore I could eat it. Good, though."

"Eggs," I said. "Fresh eggs. Marvelous."

Janey's eyes widened. "You know about them, where they comes from and all?"

"Sure: hen-fruit," I told her. She shifted her look to Harv. "Seems we ain't got to be so ashamed," she said. "If Cousin eats 'em, too."

"Would if I could get 'em," I answered her. Just then something said *spop!* I jumped, but it was just a blob of water hitting the bottom of a vinyl pail. Janey jumped up and Harv said, "Damn!" They both got busy checking the placement of the buckets, while the first spatter of rain settled down to a steady drumming. The plastic blew off one of the broken windows, and a gust of wind blew spray across the carpet. I helped Harv replace the tarp, which was pinned in place with bits of twig, jammed up tight with sticks.

"You need some nails, or tacks," I told Harv. He didn't know what those were. I told him that later I'd help him improvise, using whatever metal scraps he had. We were pretty wet and cold by then. The buckets were playing an erratic tune as the holes in the roof leaked out of harmony.

"Them damn holes," Harv muttered. "Cain't seem to get 'em sealed off."

"We'll find some tar and mend it," I told him. "That'll work better."

He nodded absently. "Whereat you learn about all those things, Cousin?"

"Used to be common knowledge."

"Sure, 'cording to what I read in them books,

lots o' things use to be common knowledge. How come you remember what ever'body else's forgot?"

"It's a long story, Harv," I told him, "and I don't quite believe it myself."

Janey gave me a second helping, along with a grateful look. "Ain't nobody ever he'ped Harv none before," she said shyly. "Glad you come, Cousin."

In the chilly evening, Harv lit up the fuel-burning furnace of the old-fashioned house. He had a modest supply of well-rotted cordwood, plus a few odds and ends of two-inch branches of later date. "Found out them tree-pieces'd burn just as good as real far-wood," he told me with pride.

"Thought they looked like the far-wood," he explained, "only smaller and not the same shape—so I tried 'em. Worked good," he added. Our breath was visible in the chilly air. "Got Janey to try em in her cook-stove, too. Cook stuff good."

I congratulated him, but later, when I saw the half-full coal-bin—half-full of coal, that is, and the other half full of junk, mostly discarded electrical or electronic appliances—and asked him why he didn't use it, he just looked puzzled.

"What fer? Cain't make nothing out of soft black rocks. Wondered why they was in there."

"They burn," I told him. "Hotter than wood." He looked at me, didn't see a grin and looked peeved.

"We're ignorant, Cousin," he remarked as if he didn't believe it. "But we know rocks don't burn. Need tree-wood for that. Told ye."

"Try it," I suggested, and I scooped up a handful of the egg-sized coals and offered them.

"Got no time fer foolishness," he said shortly.

"S'prize at ye, Cousin, tryna make a fool of me. Ain't we treated you nice?"

"*Real* nice," I agreed. "That's why I'd like to help you. Open that furnace door, and hollow out a place in the hottest part."

He hesitated, but he did it. I came over and offered the coal. "Put this on your shovel and dump it right in that pocket," I suggested. "Then watch. It'll take a few seconds to catch."

"Put the far out," he objected. I assured him it wouldn't. "This is wood, actually," I told him. "Wood that's hundreds of millions of years old. Used to be in a swamp. The trees fell and were covered with sediment, mud, you know. After a long time the sediment built up hundreds of feet deep and turned to rock, and the pressure converted the wood and leaves into coal. If you look close, you can see the impression of leaves in some of the pieces."

He picked one up, not as if he expected to see anything, and turned it over.

"Damn!" he remarked. "This here is a cattail!" He looked at me for a moment, decided not to say it, and eased the coal into the spot I'd recommended. We both watched. At first it smoked. Then little yellow-and-blue flames began licking around the black lumps. Harv turned and went to the foot of the cellar stairs and yelled for Janey; she came in a hurry, looking very worried, but he embraced her, soothed her, and told her, "Cousin here showed me something you won't hardly b'lieve," and brought her over to look in the furnace door. By then the coal was burning fiercely.

"Stones burn," he explained proudly. "We got plenty stones."

"Only the crumbly black ones," I cautioned him. " 'Coal,' it's called. You ought to be able to find plenty of it, if no one's been burning it. This is coal country."

"I know where there's a big old pile of it," Harv said, nodding. "Over by the arn strips." I realized he meant the railroad; I was beginning to accept the dialect.

"You can get enough in this bin to last a whole winter," I told him. He and Janey were both standing, gazing into the fire. The next day I showed him what the wheelbarrow in the shed was for, and we made a trek to the "arn strips." It was good to get back to the snug, warm kitchen, where Janey had a coal fire roaring in her stove, and a chicken stew ready.

28

"Cain't help wondering, Cousin," Harv said after dinner, "how it is you come to know all these things you showed us."

"I grew up in a place where everybody learned these things," I told him, not for the first time. "And lots more." I showed him some keys I'd found in a drawer, and told him what they were; he looked dubious.

"You can lock the doors when you have to go out." I went to the back door and demonstrated. He kept shaking his head; then he came over and tried the locked door. When it wouldn't open, he got upset and started shaking it and finally kicked it.

"Damn sprats can't walk in, they'll just batter it down," he said, and watched me with his mouth open as I keyed it open.

"It'll stop sneak-thieves in the night," I said. "You said you killed a boy once, in your own bedroom."

"Had to, that time," Harv muttered. "Big as me, he was. Lucky he had no knife. I brained the sucker with a chair-leg."

"You had a right," I reassured him. "But if you

lock up, nobody can get in without making a lot of noise."

The next day, I cornered a small razorback pig rooting in the chicken yard. I knocked it in the head and took it in to Janey. She recoiled, but I told her to clean it just like a chicken, and showed her how to skin it first, which made me poignantly remember the Boy Scouts and Timmy. She didn't want to touch it at first, but I suggested she think of it as a four-legged chicken and she cleaned it right up.

"It'll make a fine roast," I told her. She followed directions and that night Harv remarked on the extra-nice, but funny-looking chicken. "Got laigs onto it steada wings," he noticed. "But it's real good, Janey, don't you worry. Prob'ly one o' them mutants you hear about." He looked reassuringly at me. "Two extra laigs is better," he decided. After a while I told him what it was, and he looked more amazed than disgusted. "Know where there's plenty o' them critters at, in the woods yonder," he assured me.

"You can catch a few small ones and pen them up like your birds," I told him, "and raise 'em."

I rummaged in the pantry and found they had salt and soap and even some perished matches, but didn't know what they were for; they were delighted when I showed them. They'd been washing with fat and ashes, a combination Janey had discovered. The improvement in the omelettes when they put salt on them was much appreciated. I found a few good matches in the remains of a box, and relieved Janey of the chore of keeping hot embers in her cookstove. They seemed to think I was a supernatural being, and there was nothing credible I could tell them to explain it.

"You know, Cousin," Harv said to me one day when we were sitting on the bench in the living room, whittling some new spoons, "you favor my pa a lot. Who you say *your* pa was?"

"I didn't say," I replied. "He was Vice Admiral Timothy Jackson, USN."

" 'Timothy'!" Harv echoed. "That's funny, Cousin; my grandpa was name Timothy." Harv wagged his head. "Tough old boy, Grampa was," he mused. "Disappeared here a while back. Was a crazy, I guess: use to go in the bad place (I knew he meant Jasperton, which was taboo to these people) and watch one o' them old houses in there. Said he had to, cause some day Yupah was coming, his ma told him, he use to say. I guess the Noocler finally got him."

That blew my mind. I didn't say anything for a while.

Harv noticed and tried to be jovial. "Crazy, I guess, but he use to take me fishing. He showed me about eating live food and all. Some ways he remind me of you, Cousin."

"I'm surprised you know your family so well," I commented. "Most folks don't seem to care."

"We ain't no Silians ["civilians," I deduced]," he told me proudly. "We know, all right. 'Cept pore Janey, o' course. She was just a pore throwed-away sprat. Lucky Woman taken her in."

I couldn't figure any way to tell Harv he was my great-grandson. I tried to hint that he and Janey should have a baby, but he changed the subject. I guess that was just my genes wanting to be propagated, so I let it drop, but a day later, Janey told me in strict confidence she was afraid she was going to have a sprat. She shuddered at the word.

" 'A baby,' " I corrected her. "The greatest experience in life. Congratulations." She burst into tears and ran to tell Harv. It was the first time either of them had encountered the concept that pregnancy was anything but a disaster.

The next day, I went with Harv on an expedition to the nearby shopping mall. I made Janey listen while I explained how to use the keys to secure the house while we were gone. She dutifully locked up before we left.

It was a beautiful morning for a stroll; we cut across what had been a plowed field from which the weed-crop had been burned, and came up on the mall from behind. I didn't remember any mall being here; it must have been built just before the final collapse. It didn't look new. Back doors had been wrenched off their hinges, and litter was strewn in heaps. The looters, it appeared, had brought their finds outside, and then weeded out what they didn't want. I saw all kinds of cleaning aids, paper goods, broken ketchup and mustard bottles.

Inside it was chaos. They'd tumbled the shelving to get at the contents quicker, never mind the glass they smashed in the process. I tried to explain to Harv what some of the condiments were, and gave up. The idea that it made any difference how food *tasted* was beyond him. In the dim, chaotic interior, sealed cases, open cases, and loose cans and boxes were heaped everywhere. What

Harv was most eager to find were canned vegetables, especially any kind of beans or peas. He was guided by the pictures on the labels, which was fine until he encountered Aunt Jemima.

"Use to grind up folks, you know," he commented as he tossed the bug-infested carton aside. I didn't try to explain.

"Like this here real good," he commented, showing me a can of baked beans.

"The fresh ones are even better," I told him. He wanted to know where to get them.

"You grow them," I informed him. "Just like the stuff in your garden."

"Nope," he replied, and wagged his head. "Yer joking me, Cousin. Beans ain't green. Stuff grows is green—"

"What about carrots?" I countered. He thought that over. "Them's roots," he pointed out. "These here beans looks like peas, kinda, only pink. Got good juice."

"That's tomato sauce that gives them that color. The flavor, too."

He didn't believe me, but he let it pass.

"Where'd a feller get seeds fer them beans?" he grunted the question after a while.

"We ought to be able to find a grain and feed store," I told him. "We could find all kinds of seeds. Probably only a small percentage would still be viable, but we can try." He'd gotten accustomed to my using words he didn't understand, and had learned to deduce meaning from context.

"Seen a place once, said 'grain and feed' on it," he volunteered.

We found it: I looked around, and we filled a

battered toy wagon and two fifty-pound potato sacks with our purchases and went back out in the sunshine.

"Be nice if we could stay home and have eats jest the same," he remarked.

"Taste better, too," I agreed. "And better nutrition." We moseyed along to the hardware store, which had been pretty thoroughly looted, and managed to dig out some garden tools from under a fallen display case.

From an almost empty display of assorted knives wired to a plastic panel, I selected a penknife with a three-inch blade.

"What you want with that, Cousin?" Harv asked me. "No good in a fight, nor fer eatin', neither."

"It's for someone else," I told him.

Harv hefted a double-bitted axe and said, "Man feels better with a good weapon in his hand."

"Useful for cutting up wood, too," I reminded him. I selected a rake, with an idea of clearing the rubbish and dead weeds off Harv's lawn. He added a hoe and shovel when I explained what they were for. "When we plant those seeds, you'll need them," I pointed out.

It seemed odd that in all our expeditions, some as far as a mile from the house, we never saw anyone else foraging.

"Skeered o' the Noocler," Harv explained when I mentioned it. "Good thang, too," he went on. "Place'd been picked clean."

"Why here?" I wondered. "What's different about this patch of ground?"

He gave me one of his quizzical looks. "Funny," he remarked. "You know all kinds of stuff nobody else knows, but you don't know what ever'body knows."

"This 'Noocler,' " I responded. "What does it look like?"

"*Big*," Harv replied as if he didn't want to discuss it. "Got wings, can go anywhere, even inside, kills folks and knocks down the buildings and all."

"Why?" was my next challenge.

"Turnt," he said grumpily.

" 'Turned' what?" I kept after it.

"Never said that," Harv objected. "Said 'Turnt.' 'Noocler turnt.' "

I thought that over; finally decided it was a distortion of "nuclear deterrent." But why here? I looked out across the gone-to-weeds fields beyond the last of the partly-collapsed buildings of the Mall. Except for an abandoned car here and there or the ruins of some farm buildings, plus a scattering of young trees, there was nothing to see. The broken road curved up and over a slight rise, and a rusty sign beside it, well perforated with rusty holes, read MINIMUM SPEED 45. Harv saw me looking at it and asked,

"What's that mean, Cousin? I know the words all right, but they don't make no sense. Forty-five what?"

"Miles per hour," I told him. "They didn't want the traffic obstructed by anything going slower than that."

"You mean forty-five *miles* in a hour?" Harv didn't sound convinced. "And that's *slow*?"

"The cars could do twice that and better on a good road," I told him. "But it was against the law."

"That sounds crazy to me," Harv confided. "Ain't no wonder it all come apart. Forty-five miles in a hour," he mused. "The home place is about a mile and a half from here. Mean I could make a round trip in, uh . . ." He paused to calculate. " 'Bout two minutes," he concluded. "Man couldn't hardly set down and stand up in that time. Crazy."

As we came up over the rise, I saw below in the swale the fallen arches and broken slab of what had been the Interstate overpass. Rusted vehicles were heaped near the center, where the main span had collapsed in the midst of a traffic rush; cars and semi's coming both ways had gone over the edges and then the traffic behind had piled up. It must have been moving awful fast, evacuating Philly, probably, and then starting back when they didn't find anything encouraging in the boondocks. Harv objected to going any closer to the disaster-scene, but I insisted on getting a better look at what must have been the worst traffic accident ever.

The first skeleton was lying face-down, arm outstretched, about a hundred yards from the edge of the nearest heap of rusty metal. He'd come a long way for a fellow with a broken femur. I noticed the cuff of his hardly-rotted polyon coverall had been slashed, probably to get at his watch.

Oddly, perhaps, that was the only sign of looting I saw. Harv stood aloof and looked nervous. I went on, but he stayed put. There were skeletons in all the vehicles, and few indications of anybody having tried to depart the scene. Car doors were shut, the broken skeletons still sitting where they'd been when the car stopped moving. I went all the way to the overpass, picking a route between smashed cars. There was no indication of fire, but the base of one of the yard-square concrete supports of the main span showed blast damage. Someone had sabotaged it. Nothing I'd seen in those old newspapers could explain that, unless it had been a random act of violence by some frustrated terrorist-type. It was no wonder the place was taboo.

I went back to where Harv was waiting.

"Bad place, here, Cousin," he stated firmly when I came up, as if to discourage me from any further exploration of the site. But I'd seen enough: my idle curiosity was satisfied. I wondered briefly why Tobey hadn't sent his troops in to salvage all the copper for his buss bars. And the gold and silver jewelry, too.

Then Harv grabbed my arm. "Gotta get outa here, Cousin," he said in a tight voice. "Some bad things happen to folks comes in here." By then he was already on his way back the way we'd come, forging ahead of me. I heard a sound, and a big mastiff-like dog rushed out of a hidey-hole off to one side behind Harv and charged him silently, except for the faint sound of galloping feet on the grass. Harv heard something, turned, looked both ways, and charged the dog; it turned aside and started barking. I had my revolver out by then, but for some reason, I couldn't shoot the beast; I fired past it instead and it decided it had business elsewhere. In a moment Harv was back beside me, breathing hard, but safe, and the dog stood her ground and barked with decreasing enthusiasm. It was a bitch, obviously nursing pups. We climbed over a car, found a den with eight fat puppies in it, who came wobbling out to savor the new experience. I scooped one up and showed him to Harv.

"Cute little guy, isn't he?" I suggested.

Harv wrinkled his nose. "Damn killer," he muttered, then in spite of himself, felt of one velvety ear. "Is kind of a cute little feller at that," he conceded.

I handed him the pup and he looked it all over with great interest. "Too thin," he commented, feeling the tiny ribs. "Fatten him up on bird scraps easy."

"And he'll be your friend for life," I told him. He looked dubious.

"Any good to eat?" he asked. I told him to look into those big brown eyes and tell me what he thought. He grinned and commented,

"Don't reckon I'd like to eat him."

"Let's get a female, too," I suggested, and went back and picked one. Harv was looking at me curiously.

"Make fine watchdogs," I explained. "If you raise 'em from pups, they'll be tame."

"Reckon Janey'll like that," he commented, and we each put a pup in a pocket and went on. I felt pretty good about reestablishing man's ancient relationship with the dog. I felt a little bad for their mom, but, I told myself, she still had six.

Harv led the way off at an angle to our original route. We circled the outlying wrecks and crossed the Interstate, which was in better shape here than in most places.

From the other side I could see the straggle of

the Settlement and the stretch of regrowth woods beyond, and, in the distance the tower of the Pa—hotel. All of a sudden I was realizing that it was time to be getting back to Renada; maybe she *wasn't* OK. Tobey wouldn't soon forget that she'd not only witnessed his being locked in a closet like an erring schoolboy, but had participated in his humiliation.

I realized I had to get back—now. I told Harv I had a job to do, and that I'd see him later. I still hadn't figured out how to tell a man older than myself that I was his great-grandpa. He took it calmly, only wanted to know why he couldn't come along and he'p me. I wished him and Janey luck, handed him my pup, and told him I'd be back. Then I set off across the lumpy clods of the weed-grown acreage. When I looked back he was gone. It made me feel better to know that Pop had managed to leave his post long enough to find a wife and have a son of his own; but in the end, of course, he'd left them all to return to his duty. Quite a boy, Timmy had turned out to be.

29

As soon as I got back in the Settlement I checked on Jeannie.

Betsy came up and gave Jeannie a glance. "Too bad; she was a useful gal. Big Boy done that?" I nodded.

"Got to get outside," she told me. "Stinks too bad in here. Got my regiment to see to: You coming?" She ducked away; and I grabbed Marian's arm and told her to stand by Jeannie until I came back. I followed Betsy in time to see which way she went, and came out in a noisy mob of people armed with agricultural implements and clubs. Betsy was on a box at the far edge of the crowd, making a speech:

"All right, you mothers, we got a job o' work to do today. Want all you Silyans ta shape up in yer regular kumpnies; make a column o' platoons here, form on Humpy."

Humpy turned out to be a preternaturally tall, bony fellow whose lantern-jawed face seemed to peer out from between his shoulders. He delivered a few blows to the fellows near him, and went to stand on the pitcher's mound.

All around, other leaders were shaping up their units. In a surprisingly short time, they had sorted themselves out into ragged rectangles and files, though not without plenty of yelling, curses and blows from the harassed officers. Somebody yelled "Tenshun!" It became almost still, all across the stadium. The Man appeared, with a bustle of retainers, from an exit still marked A–70–71, and climbed up into the first row of seats. Someone set up a voice-powered mike and he intoned:

"Fellers and broads! This here is a call-to-arms from the Baron hisself, our gracious leader. This here is war! I got no time for no slackers. I hear Jersey and Dee-Cee has both of 'em gone and invaded this sacred soil o' ourn. Let's go he'p 'em pack to go home. An' remember ol' 'Basser-Sumbish' is on our side!"

Military oratory, it appeared, hadn't changed much over the years. Even the ritual yell sounded almost enthusiastic. People have always been easy to incite to wholesale mayhem.

Betsy came over and said, "Stay by me, Mister," from the side of her mouth. It was the first time she'd called me "Mister," but from there on that was my name. If there was a deep meaning in that, I failed to catch it. I followed her, though, up the ragged aisle between the muttering, 'baccy-and-weed chewing, scratching, restless columns of people dressed in a bewildering variety of make-shift clothes, with a well-preserved polyon garment here and there. Many were barefooted, or had rags bound around their feet. I wondered how they distinguished themselves from the enemy in combat, assuming the enemy troops were conscripts like themselves and not dressed like the Baron's nattily-uniformed elite troops.

Betsy was back on her box. "What we got to do," she yelled, without any preliminary call to attention, "we got to get on the main strip yonder and cut off the supplies and like that, where them suckers'll be stranded; then we can cut em up good; wouldn't want to let none of 'em starve, now." That sally was rewarded with laughter and hoots. She came back to me.

"Makin' you my adjative," she informed me.

"You mean adjutant," I replied.

"Something like that," she assented.

"What does an adjective do?" I wanted to know next.

"Stuff I ain't got the time fer," she informed me curtly. "Go over old Hump, and tell him move 'em out; and don't take no crap offen Aurelia's regiment, neither. We ain't eatin' *their* dust today."

I looked for the tall man looming above the crowd and made my way over to him. He gave me a resentful look.

"A'm'ral never tole me where I's to putt yew," he said. His voice sounded like an iron-tired cart rolling over cobblestones. Well, I never heard an iron-tired cart rolling over cobblestones or anything else, but he had a deep, rumbling voice.

"You don't 'putt' me, Humpy," I informed him. "I'm the Adjective."

His jaw dropped as far as it could. "What-all's that?"

"I'm your boss," I told him. "You just carry on, and I'll be observing."

He turned away. "Don't need no Strangy spying onto me," he muttered.

"The Baron will be glad to know you feel that way," I told him. "Now, what was that last name again?"

"Humpy's all," he rumbled. "Jest tell em 'Humpy.' Now, you fellers!" he boomed at an unfortunate pair who were wrangling over the possession of a ratty-looking plastic poncho. They both dropped it and Humpy picked it up and draped it over his own shoulders with a grand gesture. "Reckon you hearn the A'm'ral," he growled and cuffed one hard enough to send him sliding under the feet of a more disciplined squad forming up raggedly. The other fellow scuttled away and was lost in the confusion. I heard Betsy again, calling "all orfsers" together.

"All right, my bluvvid leaders, the Man hisself has got some orders fer ya!" She paused and turned expectantly toward the makeshift podium.

Bunny was back at his mike, making the ceremonial *harrumph*s and fiddling with the gadget, which emitted croaks, pops, and amplified mob-sounds.

"—hafta tell you people our Settlement here will be took from us and our lives and stuff, too, iffen we don't send the Jersey back home, bent good!" his voice boomed out, with no preliminaries.

"Git 'em 'fore they gits us," he commanded. "Any feller er gal caught fighting with one o' ourn gets kilt, right there and then," he told us. "Save it fer the enemy!"

In the relative silence after the ritual yell, Hump spoke to the man he had felled, who had gotten up and was still standing by.

"You got off easy, Sucky," he told the crestfallen fellow. "If I would of seed you couple minutes later—" He left it to Sucky's imagination.

30

Half an hour later, the whole adult population of the Settlement was on the move. There were no elderly or disabled to wave bye-bye as the column of platoons surged off toward the road. Betsy had reappeared astride an ancient red electric scooter marked "Greens Chief" and she patrolled alongside the column, stopping now and then to give orders when the column started to pack up or stretch out. I don't know what kind of admiral she was, but she was a first-class top sergeant. After the army was lined up on the road, she parked her bike and came over, looking tired but still full of pep.

"What . . . you want . . . to do now, Mister?" she panted after the brisk walk from the head of the column back to my spot at the rear, where Humpy roamed to pick up stragglers.

"We should hit the palace before dawn," I told her. "In the garage area, where the Great Troll is on guard—less defenses there—and make a big diversion so I can get across and get inside."

"You believe in that Troll stuff?" She shook her head. "Jest a tale to scare folks off."

"It's been moved," I told her. "But he has it and

215

we don't want to give him a chance to use it. So
we close in quietly, and get over the wall—then
plenty of noise. They've got fire-guns, so we need
to stay in cover as long as we can. He's got the
equipment, but we have them outnumbered. We
might be able to do it."

She nodded and went over to instruct Humpy,
just coming back with two unhappy-looking fellows. "Done a sneak, or tried to," he remarked.
"Kill 'em?" he inquired casually, and knocked their
heads together and threw them aside.

"Nope, need ever' man," Betsy told him. "Should-
n'ta slung 'em, Hump; get 'em up and moving.
Don't like the look o' Fred," she added, dubiously
eyeing the smaller of the two, who lay sprawled on
his back, with a trickle of blood from the corner of
his mouth.

Hump prodded Fred with his boot, yanked the
other one upright and shook him, eliciting a groan
and some feeble hand and foot movements. Fred
was as still as only death can make you. Betsy
snorted. "Ya gone and kilt old Fred—good scrounger,
Fred was. Throw him outer the way there, and
shape these fellers up." Then she began giving
him detailed marching orders. "Quiet, mind you,
Hump," she finished. "Don't worry about Fred
none, just get that Bob going."

Hump grumbled a little and gave me a resentful
look, but he dragged Bob away and thrust him
into the rear rank. There were some yells from up
ahead, and Betsy hurried back up to her lead
position. The whole horde started shuffling forward, with plenty of shoving and cursing and fast
retribution from the officers. Two or three fresh

corpses were expelled and lay in the ditch as object lessons to the rest.

After a while we settled down to a jerky, clumsy two miles per hour. The sun got hot, and ratty fur garments began to appear underfoot, shed by their formerly proud owners. When it cooled off tonight they'd regret that.

By mid-afternoon, the palace was looming over the trees ahead. Once, we scared up a green-uniformed detail of three men who stumbled out of a patch of woods, saw the head of the columns and, after a yell or two, turned and ran. I heard Betsy yell: "Git the mothers!" and half a dozen of our mob took off after them, overhauled them and beat them to death with shovels and clubs. They stripped the bodies and came back to Betsy grinning and trying on their new finery. Betsy yelled and they reluctantly discarded the Baron's livery.

"Can't go getting our boys mix up with the enemy," she told anybody who was listening. "Could keep one outfit," she added as an afterthought. "Send the sucker in to spy out the place."

"No good," I told her. "The mud and blood on the uniforms would tip them off before he could take three steps. We have to ease over the wall, keep out of sight, spread out all the way around the wall so they won't have a concentrated target to shoot at, then raise hell!"

"Don't know where you got to be the expert, Mister," she grumped, but she told her non-coms, "You heard him. Let's git moving."

It took a few minutes to get the column in motion again. I had to wake up some recruits who had dropped in the road, and send Hump to round up the ones who had started to wander off into the fields; then we were on the way again. I suggested to Betsy that she split the gang into columns and come up to the palace walls along two different avenues. She OK'd that, and took one bunch; I had the other, with Hump as *my* adjective.

We reached the wall only a few yards from where Pop and I had first scaled it, and I briefed Hump, who briefed the noncoms, and pretty soon I saw Betsy's bunch come up on the parallel street, and over we went. It was quiet inside, and the troops did a good job of keeping it that way. They didn't ask any questions as to why we were attacking when we had come to help.

I prowled along the wall to my left, and helped a few fellows find good concealment as far forward as was practical. I had a good view of the palace from a clump of junipers. The old building loomed up aloof against the blue and white sky. Renada was in there, safe and sound and waiting for me, I told myself. Tobey was nuts, but he wouldn't really take it out on the girl he'd raised—I hoped.

I watched the fringe of foliage along the wall to the left and right and saw nothing that would arouse the curiosity of the guards. A sentry was pacing the terrace near where I planned to make my try, but he was only walking the prescribed pattern, unconcerned. I waited the ten minutes Betsy and I had agreed on, and just as I was about to utter my signal yell, I heard Betsy's from way over on the other side of the garages. The sentry halted, listened, started toward the yell, then heard another, closer, and changed course toward it. One of our men, a tall fellow, broke from concealment and charged the sentry, who skidded to a halt and drew his pistol. He fired three times into the tall rebel before they collided, and only the tall man got up. It was Big Boy. He tried to run back to the line, but he tripped over his own feet and didn't move when slugs slammed into him from concealment. Tough to the end, Big Boy was.

I could see a few others moving up now, and I worked my way over to the outlying hedge behind which I planned to knee-and-elbow my way up to the palace. After another half-minute of inconspicuous activity, our boys settled down again, well out of sight, but making plenty of noise. More of the green-clad guard-force had come at a run from the garage area and were spreading out, rifles at the ready, looking for something to shoot at. A few fell to arrows. The boys kept up intermittent noises from widely scattered points, and after a while the guards drew together, pointed to a spot in the perimeter shrubbery chosen, apparently, at random, and charged, firing as they went. A man staggered into view directly in their path, bloody, and fell under a new fusillade.

Nobody was looking my way; I kept moving up. When the Greenies reached the shrubbery between the trees, they plunged in. I heard a few shots and lots of threshing, and nobody came out. Now more men in green were coming up, running in every direction; now and then one veered into the shadowy mass of foliage along the perimeter wall and didn't come out.

By then I was in position for my final rush; there were no guards close. I hit the dirt and scuttled over to the big bush covered with white berries that was the terminus of the hedge, and dived behind it. A slug kicked dirt over my feet as I pulled them in, but I hugged the ground, well in under the hedge, and nothing else happened.

Disorganized Greenie guards were still running in various directions; none of our boys were in sight, except a few dead. There were scattered shots and plenty of yelling, but no indication of any penetration of the line by the guards. The Grand Army didn't look like much, but they caught on quick, with all that loot in the offing. Off to the left, I saw Hump come across the corner at a run, right on the heels of a guard officer. I averted my eyes, but I heard the strangled yell.

I came in along an unpaved path behind the base plantings I'd noticed from the windows of the baronial suite. The lights were on there now. I wondered if that was a good sign or not.

I passed the rotted-out steel garbage bins and kept close to the wall, behind the dense base plantings, and found the small service door I had assumed the path would lead me to. It was locked hard, but I used my pocket toolkit to remove one hinge. Then I levered the edge of the sheet-metal–clad panel out far enough for me to get a two-handed grip and heave hard. The other hinge broke and the door fell outward, not without enough noise to alert anybody within fifty feet, but nobody came.

It was pitch-dark inside, but I knew the layout roughly from my previous snooping in the kitchen area. Once past the aroma of well-rotted compost, I detected the same kitchen smells I'd smelled before. I eased ahead. It was silent; no Grand Ball in progress tonight. The rest was a matter of sneaking a few yards, listening, tiptoeing some more. I skirted the pantry area and found the grand staircase and went up. Once or twice I heard voices in the distance and froze, but they didn't come any closer. I reached the third floor and scouted the layout.

It was strangely quiet, considering the excitement outside. I tried the big gold-plated doorknob and stepped inside.

31

Renada was standing by the tall window, looking out at the floodlit lawn. She turned quickly as I came in. The strange-looking gun in her hand was aimed at my chest; she threw it aside and came to me. She was slim and cool and satiny and smelled good. Her hair was smooth and glossy. She'd come a long way from that garbage can. I held her tightly, then leaned back to look at her face. It was unmarked. She looked out into the night.

"I came as quick as I could," I told her.

"Of course, Jack." She shuddered. "When that Pig-Eye took you away, I was afraid," she said quietly.

"Me, too," I told her, making light of two murders.

She stepped back abruptly and looked me in the face. "Did you see Bud and Marian?" she asked uncertainly.

"I sure did. Great people; they asked about you."

"Amidst all the hate and greed out there," she said, "they were the only unselfish ones." She turned back to me. "Can't we do something for them?" she pleaded. "You have no idea . . ."

"Maybe I do. Certainly we'll do something."

"If the food and clothing supplies were organized . . ." she suggested. "And so much more."

"Do you have a good doctor here in the palace?" I thought to ask. "And a dentist?"

She nodded uncertainly. "Colonel Stanley is Tobey's personal quack," she said, and turned to me again. "Why? Do you have a toothache? Is Marian sick, or Bud?"

"Not especially," I countered. "But there are others."

"Of course," she agreed. "I was being selfish, I'm afraid."

"Just what did they do for you to earn such devotion?" I asked, remembering the cold and rapacious pair I'd met.

"They fed me," she said, starry-eyed. "They gave me clothes—and they kept the terrible men away. Then—the Greenies caught me, and I didn't even have an opportunity to say goodbye." Her eyes were fixed on mine. She must have read something there, or thought she did. Her face lit up like dawn over a misty garden. "What Tobey was saying," she blurted. "About using the old ship to restore the magic—the electricity, I mean— could we really do it?"

"Since Tobey said so," I told her, "I think so. He was our electronics wizard. He helped design the energy sink. He said it was all set to go—but first there are the men still aboard."

"How exciting!" she said, already seeing it accomplished. "How wonderful for Day and Macy and Dalton! To live again, after all these years! And they can help us!" She caught my hands.

"With all their knowledge and training, they'll help us show the people how to really live again!"

"I can think of worse tutors for humanity than a crowd of astronauts," I conceded. But the ship—the magnificent *Prometheus*. Man's greatest accomplishment. The embodiment of human aspiration and technology. To abort the mission when I could save it . . . It was even possible, with some luck, that we could plant a viable colony—a fresh start for humanity. Humanity *needs* a fresh start, I thought.

Renada was looking out at the dark lawn again. There were still a few blue flashes from energy weapons, firing outward. Greenies: they were close, clear of the perimeter and moving in, retreating.

"We'll have to stop this," I told Renada. "Can you contact the head of the Guard Force and tell him to cease fire?" She nodded and went into the next room. I followed her. It was a small command-post type chamber, packed with comm gear and LED displays. She was already talking into a box in the center of the main panel: "Colonel Powell; Green One to Green Two: terminate deadly force at once. Hold them, but cease firing. Use the Divine Wind." She turned to me. "That's what Tobey calls his knockout gas system. I've sealed us off."

At one side, a crude wooden mounting held a heavy-duty circuit-breaker. Inch-thick cables led away from it.

"That's Tobey's greatest treasure," Renada told me. "It has something to do with the ship and the magic."

"Certainly," I said. "It must control a relay that

activates his power-plant scheme—after the change-over at the ship."

"He used to stand and gaze at it," Renada remarked. "If we used it now . . ."

"I wouldn't do a thing until the change-over is made aboard ship," I reminded her. "After landing on Callisto, we were supposed to make the change-over to enable us to use the coil for ground-power. He's wired this cutout into the circuits. Then he, only *he* could control the magic."

"And now—" Renada's hand clutched my arm.

"We'll see," I assured her. "How do we make contact with the guard commander?"

"After order is restored," she volunteered, "I've arranged for Powell to come up and let us know, personally."

"You're sure he's to be trusted?" I asked dubiously.

"I saved his life—besides, he's sweet on me," she remarked casually.

"How will he feel about your spending a few days and nights locked in here alone with me?"

"That's a thought," she admitted, not unhappily. "Perhaps we'd better slip out."

"Both sides will be shooting at us," I mentioned. "Let's go."

"First you need food and rest," she decreed. "We'll go tomorrow; after all, Tobey's not going to go anywhere without his guard."

I was in no mood to argue the point.

We dined on palace-reared chicken and fresh potatoes and gravy. It was the best meal I'd ever had. Afterward, she showed me the guest room. I started toward the actual bed, and I don't remember anything until I woke up with a cold cloth on my face and a warm voice in my ears.

"It's been quiet for three hours now," Renada was telling me. "I told Powell I needed a little more rest. Wake up, Jack, it's time to go." I remember something about a hot bath after that.

She showed me a nice new powder-blue uniform like the one I'd taken off the Jersey colonel, but with less gold braid. "You're a major," she told me. It was a bust in rank, but I didn't ask any silly questions; it was clean and dry and it fit pretty well. I managed to go to the toilet all by myself, and the moment had come to make our try. Renada was fetchingly clad in a riding outfit, complete with snazzy boots and a holstered firearm. She looked me in the eyes in that disconcerting way of hers. "Things are quiet; we can slip out now." I nodded.

"We *will* abort the mission?" she asked and told me.

"We'll see," I replied. I thought about *Prometheus* as she'd be as the centuries went by, and she lay quiescent in the earth, her systems still intent and counting, her autobrain perhaps wondering what was wrong . . .

32

Later, in the passage leading to the garages, she told me, "Colonel Powell said it's more or less a stalemate. He has his men dug in in the cellar, with plenty of supplies. The rebels stopped to loot the ground floor; they're still at it, bogged down there. The colonel managed to convince everybody that Jersey came in on his side and tried to take over, and he fooled them."

"Swell," I commented. "So both sides will think I'm a spy, in this pretty getup."

"I couldn't help it," she told me. "It was in Tobey's personal collection of loot. His own clothes wouldn't fit you, of course. We can go back and try to find something else for you to change into if you want to."

I shook my head; my thoughts were on other matters. "You mean Powell had already foxed everybody before you talked to him," I guessed. "I thought it was something he'd come up with on our account."

"Not at all; he had a mutiny on his hands, and he dressed a few men in captured blue and convinced his troops Jersey had sent them to help. Then he released a prisoner to spread the word among the rebels. It all just got out of hand. He told me, to explain why he couldn't just let me come out and join the victory celebration. He thinks Tobey is dead, and he doesn't know about you."

"And I thought this was going to be the easy part."

33

It was a long walk in the dark down one of Tobey's trick secret passages, and the dust made both of us sneeze, but nobody came to investigate: the Grand Army's attack had disrupted the Baron's tight security. We made it to the narrow little door that opened into a dark corner of the garage.

I eased out and waved Renada back. Low-pockets was still on duty. He saw me loom up out of the shadows and hesitated; he'd seen me before, but couldn't quite place where, but when I came out into better light, my pretty blue suit with the gold leaves on the shoulders stopped him. He backed off and I stalked across to a vast black Bentley—an early 20's model, I guessed, from the maglev suspension. I popped the door open. The gauge showed three-quarters full charge. I opened the glove box, rummaged, found nothing. But then it wouldn't be up front with the chauffeur . . .

I worked the button to open the back door. There was a crude black-leather holster riveted against the smooth pale-gray leather door pad, with the butt of a 4mm showing. There was another on the opposite door, and a power rifle was slung from straps on the back of the driver's seat.

Tobey was overcompensating for his insecurity. I searched the shadows behind me for Renada, spotted her in the lee of a half-track, motioned her over. She came up and I held the back door for her. She slipped in and sat on the roomy, leather-smelling seat, and unshipped the rifle. I took a pistol, tossed it onto the front seat, and slid in beside it. An apprentice mechanic gaped at me as I eased my sprained left arm into my lap and twisted to close the door.

I started up; there was a bad solenoid somewhere, but she ran all right. I eased her forward and flipped a switch, and cold lances of light speared out into the rain, lighting the car-yard like a stage set. At the last instant, the attendant started forward with his mouth open to say something discouraging, but I didn't wait to hear it. I gunned out into the night, swung into the graveled drive, and headed for the gate. Mallon had had it all his way so far, but maybe it still wasn't too late . . .

Two sentries looking miserable in shiny black ponchos stepped out of the guard hut as I pulled up. One peered in at me, started to say something; then his eyes went to Renada in the back, and he came to a sloppy position of attention and presented arms. Mama-brass still had its privileges. I moved my foot to the go-pedal and the second sentry called something. The first sentry looked startled, and started to swing the gun down to cover me. I floorboarded it; the Bentley roared off into the dark along the potholed road that led into town. I thought I heard a shot behind me, but I wasn't sure.

"First," I told Renada, "I have to check on

Jeannie. Betsy promised to come back and find her and watch over her as well as she could."

"Of course," Renada said. "We can go to the site afterward."

"There used to be a pretty good farm road along here," I said. I didn't mention that I was having a hard time telling just where I was with all the cheery billboards fallen, and the road signs cut up for weapon-steel long ago. But I spotted my side road, and swung in, slamming over the ruts and gullies, which the big Bentley's suspension smoothed out to just a slightly bumpy glide. The yellow lights of the Settlement were visible ahead, not doing much to relieve the blackness. There was enough pale moonlight to show me the general lay of the land, and the big car's twin blue-white beams defined every pebble in the weed-grown trail.

I pulled off on a side trail where they used to turn tractors around or something, and braked to a halt. I hated the idea of getting out of that plush warmth into what was waiting outside, but I thought of little Jeannie after all this time of the kind of care she'd be getting from Bunny's yahoos, and I opened the door to an icy blast.

Renada got out first and checked the action on the power-gun. I climbed out, distributed the rest of the arsenal between us, and told Renada: "The trick is to not use these. They're fine for bluff, but in a shoot-out, there's too many of them."

Renada shuddered. "I don't want to kill anyone," she said in a stony voice.

"Neither do I, I assure you," I said, feeling a little miffed. "But there's about sixteen hundred wild primates up ahead who'd love to kill *us*. So we have to be prepared."

I was talking to myself; Renada was no stranger to the realities of life in what was left of Nice Day.

I looked around, located the rusty water tower, and led the way across to it.

When we were twenty feet away, Betsy's voice came softly: "That you, Mister?"

"The password is 'Jeannie,' " I said. "I have a friend with me."

"Seen they was two of ye," Betsy came back. "Jeannie's doin' okay. Not as purty, but okay. Got Hump watchin' her. And a female name of Finette's he'ping, too. Doing for her. Cost me some extra rations I had."

I made brief introductions, was glad to see no sign of female rivalry, and got Betsy's briefing. She had Jeannie fixed up pretty well in the Spittle, a shack where they took folks fixing to die, she explained. "On'y Jeannie ain't dyin'. Just a little trouble breathin' was all. Old Medic come by once and wanneda mess with her but I run him off after he pulled that bloody gauze outa her nose. She can breathe good now." I took Renada's hand and followed Betsy when she set off into the dark.

We were coming up on the Settlement from the south, with the wind at our backs, so the stink wasn't overpowering. The rooting swine grumbled and got out of the way. The stray chickens *buc-buc*'ed and skittered off in the darkness. Man's old domesticates had adapted to the rich, full life of the free. This had been a public park in the old days, I remembered, where the folks who came for the football game could have a picnic lunch and give the dog a run before forcing their way into the grandstands. The big old oaks and elms were still here, but the grass had been replaced by knee-high weeds; still, it was fairly easy going. We came up to the first cluster of huts, dim in the waning moonlight. Nobody challenged us. "Where's the Spittle from here?" I whispered the question to Betsy.

"Yonder," she called over her shoulder. "Ain't far." She set off at an angle to the previous route and went in between a collapsing vinyl jet-engine case and a falling-down tent, each apparently housing a dozen or so argumentative individuals, judging from the snarls and snips of cantankerous conversation:

"—hand offen me, you ape . . ."

"—my spot, got it all warmed up."

"Don't know where *you* come from; git off!"

"Them's *my* stash. Looky here, Blinky, this here feller is stealing stuff!"

I heard the meaty sound of a blow and a small, wiry fellow came reeling out of the tent and fell at my feet. He lay there and stared at my boots for a moment, then scrambled up, wiping his mouth with the back of his forearm. He groped inside his ratty fur jacket and came out with a rusty can with no label.

"I was *going* to put it back, I just wanneda *look* at it! Been so long since I et good, I guess I musta went offa my chump for a minute there, Cap'n!"

I pushed him aside. "Keep it," I told him.

I saw Joey's dirty face peering at me from between tent shreds and motioned him over. He disappeared and reappeared beside me. He was as

agile as a snake. I felt for the knife, thought I'd
lost it, then felt it down in the corner of my
pocket. I handed it to the boy. He looked puzzled,
then I showed him how to open the blade.

"That's just right for whittling, Joey," I explained.
"But no good for sticking into people."

"Aw, I don't wanna stick nobody anyways," he
said, as if explaining to himself. He darted a quick
look at my face. "Ain't took nothing from nobody,
like you said," he muttered, as close as he could
come to thanking me. I told him that was good,
and asked him to show me what he whittled. He
nodded and damn near grinned before he darted
away.

I plodded on, keeping Betsy barely in sight
ahead.

"We must get your friend Jeannie to the palace," Renada said, with a shudder in her voice.

I squeezed her hand. "First we have to find
her," I pointed out.

"C'mon over this way," Betsy said and set off
without waiting for any discussion; then she slowed.
"Careful, here."

The little thief was right at my heels. "Wait a
minute, Strangy," he whispered. "You don't wanna
go nowhere near the Spittle; went over myself to
get some easy pickin's from some o' them as is
dying and don't need no grub. Old Hump, he nigh
kilt me. See, I got this year bruise pra'tic'ly glows
in a dark.

"You treated me good, Strangy," he went on.
"Wanta do ya a good turn. You're cold and wet,
what you need, you needa get inside where it's

warm, and get some eats. Come on, I'll show you a crazy *gives* eats away!"

Betsy came back to see what all the whispering was about. "Oh, that's old Frankie and Finette yer talkin' about," she said. "Might be a good idear at that. You, Weasy, you get in front." She pushed the little man ahead.

"Old Frank and Finette ain't been here all their lives," she told me and Renada, who had come up beside me to listen.

"I've heard of them," Renada commented. "I remember when they came: strange people from Dee-Cee, I understand. They started helping the sick ones. They had a hard time: people used to throw stones at them because they didn't trust anybody so crazy. Then later I got to know them a little. They were strange, but good. I helped them, until Marian caught me one day."

The cold was getting to my bones: I imagined frost forming on them.

"Their eats is good," Weasy stated, and forged ahead.

I pulled Renada over to whisper to her. "Is there really someone here who's giving food away?"

"I don't really remember that part," she told me. "I was only a child, but I think it was something like that. Scary."

"Maybe there's hope for us after all," I remarked.

About that time, Betsy came back and said, "You two wait here. Weaz and me'll go ahead and see what's up." She moved away silently. The fine, misty rain was turning to sleet. It worked its way down my neck; I helped Renada tug her furs closer around her ears.

"We have to get in out of this," I said. "It's close to freezing, and with the sleet and the wind-chill we'll be into hypothermia in a matter of minutes."

She squeezed my gloved hand. "Hush," she said, and Betsy bustled up and said, "C'mon, it's all set."

She led the way along a shallow gully where dirty ice-water gurgled, to a bigger-than-average hut where Weazy was working his way around behind a man and woman dressed in well-worn factory-made clothes who were trying to secure the flapping edge of a tarp that sort of covered one wall of the hut. Weazy waited for his chance, when the struggling couple went around to the other side to secure another tarp. Then he squatted and snaked a hand under the flapping edge and came out with a number ten can. I stepped on his wrist and he squalled and kicked at me. Just then Frank and Finette came back. Frank, who was short and burly, grabbed Weazy by the arm and threw him bodily backward into a splash of mud and water. He tossed the can back under the tent-edge and stood to face me.

"Thanks, Brother," he muttered, as if not wanting to overhear himself. The woman, who was also sturdy-looking, with a worn, pretty face, came over to Renada and said, "Betsy sez yer our Rennie come back. Good. Feared ye'd come to grief. I need yer help here." She turned away and Renada followed, and I followed Renada.

The entry was covered by a sodden canvas. We continued into a stink that was perhaps slightly less pungent than that outside. There were people lying on the dirt floor between puddles. Our host-

ess checked and began moving battered pots from
one drip to another. A man groaned and grabbed
her ankle. She looked down at him and said, almost inaudibly under the drumming of rain on
canvas, "I'll get to you, Scratch. Be patient a little
longer."

"Cain't, Finny!" the man said in a deep, wheezy
voice. "Fetch Frank. I got to go bad!"

The woman turned to Renada and spoke to her.
Renada nodded and went back to the fly to urge
Frank on.

"Finette needs you," she told him as he came
in, dripping. He paused to squeegee water from
his forehead with a blunt forefinger while he took
in the situation. He went to the man on the floor,
caught his arm and hauled him to a sitting position. "Come on, Scratchy, get on yer feet! You can
he'p some. Got no call to make me carry ye!"

Scratch complained but got his feet under him
and Frank led him out into the drizzle. I followed,
with a vague idea of helping Frank with whatever
he had to do. As soon as the stocky man cleared
the tent-hut, half leading and half carrying Scratch,
Weazy eased in behind him and raised what looked
like a stick. I caught his arm and the length of steel
pipe fell. Frank turned and said quietly, "I tole
you don't hang around here, Weazy. Yer knee is
knitted up, yer all right now. We done all we
could fer ye. Go and do a scrounge fer yerself."

Weazy started to whine and bluster, at the same
time trying to get into position to kick me. I
waited until he thought he was all set; then swept
his feet from under him and put a foot on his chest
to hold him in place. He subsided, except for

some muttering. I caught "—kill the both of ye!" and ". . . feller can't even sleep in his own nest!"

"He'ped you all we could, Weasel," Frank told him. "Tole ya that. Bone's healed good, need the space fer somebody *needs* it."

While this was going on, Scratch had proceeded a few feet and clumsily squatted to relieve himself. He rose abruptly, shouldered his way past Frank and me, and reentered the hut. The wind was tugging relentlessly at the torn canvas above the entry. It ripped another six inches as I watched it. A man was crouched at the far side of the ramshackle structure. Frank saw him and said, "You get away from that, Pud! I told you before. Now go on, git! You're a big healthy mother, git on, now, and tend to yer own!"

Pud gave him a pained look, and grabbed the tear in the roof and tore it another foot. "You going to make me, Frankie?" he yelled. "Yew ain't going to do nothing! You're too dumb to know when yer being stoled from, and ain't got the sand to do nothing about it iffen ye *did* know!" He advanced in an insolent strut.

Somehow, I had taken a dislike to Pud. I used the pipe I had taken from Weazy to slap him across the front of his waterlogged coat. He gave me an astonished look and turned and ran off, blundering against huts and tents, eliciting yells in his wake.

"That's a mean one, Felly," Frank told me. "Fixed his haid once where somebody parted his hair with a two-by-four. Bled some, I tell ye."

"I've seen plenty like him," I told Frank. "They

regard kindness as stupidity, and courtesy as weakness."

Frank nodded. "Hard to he'p a feller like that," he commented. "Better get back inside 'fore old Scratch needs out again. Keep telling him not to eat the rotten stuff."

Back in the slightly warmer and drier interior, I found Renada deep in conversation with Finette. She reached out to take my hand at the same time she greeted Frank. "Jack, this is Frank and Finette, my friends. Folks, Lieutenant Commander Jackson. He was a friend of Commander Banner."

They took the anachronism calmly and Frank urged me over to a drier corner under a hard plastic panel that kept the rain off pretty well, and seated me on a plank seat before an improvised table. Finette set out opened cans and some almost clean spoons.

"Not much, but times is hard," Frank muttered. " 'Friend o' Mander Banner,' eh?" he mused and looked at me curiously. He had a tough, square face with scars, and a few broken teeth, and ratty-looking reddish hair.

"You tell her that, felly, or what?"

I nodded. "He was her grandfather," I mentioned.

"Great-grandpa," Frank corrected. "Grandpa was Tol; knowed him as a boy. Fine old man."

I remembered a runny-nosed kid named Tolliver, the son of a physicist on the Mission. He used to hang around with Timmy. I let it drop. There was too much to remember and wonder about.

"You look good, fer over a hundred," Frank told me, keeping an eye on me for my reaction. Finette shushed him.

"Commander Jackson was in a state of suspended animation for over eighty years," Renada said. "He was awakened when the automatic controller detected trouble. He's here to help us. We're on our way to the Forbidden Place, to do wonderful things he knows how to do, to make everything better."

Frank and Finette listened to that in silence. If they believed it, they didn't say so. It was my time to do some shushing. "Don't try to explain, kid," I told Renada. "After it's done will be soon enough. Meanwhile, what about Jeannie?"

"Got her in the back," Finette said. "She's gonna be all right. Poor little thang. So purty, she was. Good thang somebody helped her, she'd a been daid now." She gave me a sidelong glance. "Yew the one he'ped her?" She asked it as if it were a mildly disgraceful secret.

"I did what I could," I told her. "Medic packed her nose."

Frank snorted. "Taken what she had on her while he was doin' it, too, I bet. Had to run the skunk off from the Spittle, here."

"I didn't see him steal anything except a quick feel," I replied. By that time we were back in the darkest corner of the noisome Spittle. I saw Jeannie lying on her side, her head bandaged with dirty rags, her eyes open. I could sense her smile through the rags.

I said, "Hello, Jeannie. How are you feeling?" Hump was standing a few feet beyond her. He took a step toward me just as Betsy came up.

"Howdy, girl," she muttered. "Saw old Boy get it in the battle," she added. "One tough son of a wild sow. He won't be hitting no girls no more."

I knelt beside the girl. "Jeannie," I said, trying to be gentle, "you'll have to get up now and come with us. We're going to take you to a nice warm, dry place with a real bed, and plenty of hot food. Then you can sleep." What I could see of her face was one large purple-black bruise. Her eyes were puffy.

"Teeth is broke," she said and touched them with the tip of her tongue. "Cain't eat anyways."

"We can even fix that," I reassured her, thinking of Tobey's pet dentist.

Renada went around to the other side of the pallet and helped her to her feet. She was weak but she made it. I told Hump we'd take good care of her.

"He'p her good, Adjective," he growled. "Like little Jeannie good. Nice to me."

34

Between Renada and me, Jeannie was able to stay on her feet and even work them a little. The sound of Tobey's convoy was audible from the Settlement now; it was passing on the state road that passed on the other side of the shantytown. That helped, because everybody was looking that way at the troll-lights, muttering to each other about magic spells; lots of them were kneeling in the mud doing fancy rituals, complete with gestures and outcries. They were too busy being scared to pay any attention to me and the two women. We bypassed the fallen water-tank and followed the track to where we'd left the Bentley. It was undisturbed; I helped Jeannie in, and after Renada got Betsy inside, over her objections (she was pretty worried about the demons out in the night), it started right up and we got to the strip that used to be State 35, at which point Betsy demanded to get out. She had to see to her battalion, which had suffered twenty percent casualties. She waved hesitantly and disappeared in the misty rain.

"She was—is a fine woman," Renada said. "She told me her great-grandfather was Mander Black.

245

She has mementos of his." She was slumped in the seat, barely awake.

I took the river road south of town, pounding at reckless speed over the ruined blacktop, gaining on the lights of Mallon's horde paralleling us a mile to the north. After a quarter mile, the Bentley blew a shock and skidded into a ditch. I sat for a moment taking deep breaths to drive back the compulsive drowsiness that was sliding down over my eyes like a visor. Renada got out and came up to sit beside me. My arm throbbed like a cauterized stump. I needed a few minutes' rest . . . My head drooped over onto Renada's shoulder.

35

Jeannie was moaning in her sleep. Renada got
in back to try to make her more comfortable. I got
the Bentley back up on the road, limping with its
left rear corner low, but still plenty of car. I had to
give some thought to which way to go. With the
window open, I could hear the convoy passing,
not far away. Harv and Janey's place was in the
opposite direction; that decided me.

"I'm going to take her to a safe place," I told
Renada, and answered her questions. She agreed
it was a good idea. I got us moving via the route
I'd figured out, and in ten minutes, driving without lights, I made it to the Interstate, where I
could make a little better time, but not for long—
the fallen overpass was only a couple of miles east.
I took the exit before it, a pretty fair road that
curved out and around the area of the traffic pile-up,
to the disintegrated secondary road Harv and I
had used on our trip to market. Mallon's convoy
was barely audible here. It was a bumpy five-
minute drive to the Jackson residence, which I
could barely see in the light of a gibbous moon,
and pulled up behind the chicken yard. There was
a light in the kitchen. I told Renada to wait where

247

she was with Jeannie while I tried to do a sneak approach. No doubt the Jacksons were on the alert, what with the sounds of the convoy, faint but audible here.

When I was fifty feet from the kitchen door, Harv moved out into the path I was following, the Webley in his hands.

"Easy, Harv," I called softly. "It's only me, needing a favor, as usual."

"Come outa there, Cousin—I mighta shot ye!" he responded. "What's going on? What's all the noises from the palace-way?"

"Just Tobey Mallon, conquering the world," I told him, and came up into the light from the window. Harv lowered the shotgun. "Come on inside, boy; Janey's skeered, me coming out here, but we heard some o' that funny noise coming this way; then it stopped. Right relieved it's you," he confessed, and put a forearm across his face. "Tard," he explained. "Long day, Cousin. Let's go in and eat. What was that I heard sneaking up on the strip?"

"That was a car," I told him. "I swiped it from the Baron. I'll show you tomorrow. Right now, I've got an injured young girl with me. She's not in danger of dying, but she needs care. I thought maybe Janey—"

"Let's get her inside," he said, as if grumpily. I told him about Renada, and she met us ten feet from the car.

"Jeannie's a little delirious," she said before I could make introductions. We got her out of the car, over her feeble objections, and Harv ducked and picked her up as if she were a feather bolster.

He was his grandpa's grandson, all right. We trailed him along to the back door, where Harv called quietly to Janey, who opened up and came out to start fussing over Jeannie. By the kerosene light in the kitchen, Jeannie looked like a badly embalmed mummy in her dirty bandages, and even Renada looked weary and drawn. The Jacksons rustled some hot cereal (which I'd shown them how to fix) and coffee (ditto) and got Jeannie fixed up on a nearly intact mattress, where she immediately went into a sound sleep.

Janey and Renada had a lot to talk over, and I gave Harv a condensed account of the mission we were on. He mostly looked at me with an expression between incredulity and amazement, but he let me finish.

". . . so you can see," I told him, "we have to get moving now. Afterward, I'll come back and bring you up to date."

"Wait a minute," Harv said. "You tryna tell me we're gonna have the magic back? All this junk machinery is gonna start working all at once? Don't know as I'd favor that, Cousin."

"It won't work until you turn it on," I reassured him. "After you get used to it, you'll wonder how you ever did without it. There'll be bugs to iron out," I cautioned, "maybe big ones. We'll have to play it by ear."

Harv wanted to know what that meant, about the ear and all, but I had to decline to try to explain music to people who'd never heard any. "That will be one of the great things," I told them, as Renada got back into her now somewhat drier furs.

"You mean"—Harv looked puzzled—"people sit around and listen to a machine making noises? That's all?"

"You'll understand when you hear it," I assured him; then, with a final handshake and a hug for Janey, we went back out into the cold, wet night. Harv stayed behind, at my insistence. I warned them to lie low if anyone else came around in a motor vehicle, and we parted.

36

Staying to a back road Harv had reminded me of, I had a better chance to beat Mallon to the site. It was quiet going for a while; then a sound brought me alert like an old maid smelling cigar smoke in the bedroom; the not-very-distant rise and fall of heavy engines in convoy. Mallon was coming up at flank speed. The Bentley was an obvious target; we got out in the rain and headed off along the wet shoulder at a trot. Our chances had been as slim as a gambler's wallet all along, but if Mallon could beat us to the objective, they dropped to nothing; still we didn't have far to go, and he was sticking to the road.

The eastern sky had taken on a faint gray tinge against which I could make out the silhouetted gateposts and the dead floodlights only a hundred yards ahead. The roar of engines was getting louder, fast. I could make out the howl of the Bolo's gyros over the din. There were other sounds, too: the chatter of 9mm's, the *boom!* of falling masonry. With his new toy, Mallon was not going around obstacles; he was dozing his way through the men and buildings that got in his way.

The rain slacked off a little as we reached the

fence; we picked a way over fallen wire mesh, then headed for the Primary Site. We couldn't run here. The broken slabs tilted crazily, in no pattern. Renada was having a hard time, holding onto my good arm for support. She slipped, stumbled, but I kept my feet and so did she. Behind us, the Bolo's polyarc beams threw ink-black shadows across the slabs. Ours jittered ahead of us. It wouldn't be long before someone spotted us and opened up with the guns . . .

The whoop! *whoop!* WHOOP! of the guardian Bolo cut across the field. I saw the two red eyes flash, sweeping our way. I told Renada to keep down. Back near the gate, dust boiled above a massed rank of battered old vehicles drawn up in battalion front just beyond the old perimeter fence, engines idling, ranged for a hundred yards on either side of the wide gap at the gate. I looked for the high silhouette of Mallon's Bolo, saw it far off down the avenue, decked out in red, white, and green navigation lights, a jeweled dreadnought. The glaring cyclopean eye at the top darted a blue-white pencil of light ahead, swept over the waiting escort, outlined me like a set-shifter caught onstage by the rising curtain.

The *whoop! whoop!* sounded again behind us. The automated sentry Bolo was bearing down on us along the lane of light. Even if it couldn't fire a gun, those treads could squash us as flat as yesterday's beer. I grabbed at the plastic disk in my pocket as though holding it in my hand would somehow heighten its potency. I didn't know if the Lesser Troll was programmed to exempt me

from destruction or not, and there was only one
way to find out . . .

It wasn't too late to make a run for it. Mallon
might shoot—or he might not. I could convince
him that he needed me, that together we could
grab twice as much loot . . .

I wasn't really considering it; it was the kind of
thought that flashes through a man's mind like
heat lightning when time slows in the instant of
crisis, but it was just a thought—one I didn't like
having. Renada was just about done. I helped her
up, and made a few more yards with her feet
dragging, found a hollow between slabs and got
her down into it. She'd be as safe here as anybody
could be under the guns of an angry Bolo. She
moaned and opened her eyes. I gave her a grin I
didn't feel. She smiled back.

"Wait here and keep down," I told her. "I'll be
back for you."

She nodded and hunkered down; her furs would
keep her warm, and the Greenies wouldn't notice
her. She was a capable gal—and a brave one,
trusting me. It was my turn to do something to
justify that trust. It was hard to be smart feeling as
bad as I did, but what I had to do didn't really
take courage. I was a small, soft, human grub,
stepped-on but still moving, caught on the chaos
of broken concrete, between the clash of chrome-
steel titans—but I knew which direction to take.
The Lesser Troll rushed me in a roll of thunder
and I gave Renada what I hoped was a reassuring
look and went to meet it.

It stopped twenty yards from me, looming massive as a cliff. Its heavy guns were dead, I knew.

That must have been quite a fight, twenty years ago, before the Mark II withdrew, to have drained its reserves so low. I could see the battle damage on its prow: craters in the flint-steel armor from futile hard-shots, plus plenty of pits made when the surface metal boiled under the energy beams. Without its main armament it was no more dangerous than a farmer with a shotgun—

But against *me*, now, a shotgun was enough. The slab under me trembled as if in anticipation. I squinted against the dull red IR beams that had pivoted to hold me, waiting for eternity, or half a second, while the Troll considered. Then the guns elevated, pointed over my head like a benediction. The Bolo knew me.

The guns traversed fractionally; I looked back toward the enemy line, saw the Great Troll coming up now, closing the gap, towering over its escort like a planet among moons. And the twin infinite repeaters of the Lesser Troll tracked it as it came—the empty guns that for twenty years had held Mallon's scavengers at bay.

The noise of engines was suddenly louder now; the lesser war-cars were regrouping; the Mark III came on slowly, pulverizing old concrete under its churning treads. Lights sparkled along the line of combat vehicles, but I didn't realize I was being fired on until I saw chips fly to my left, and heard the howl of the ricoshays. It was time to move. Renada was safe, off to the side. I scrambled around under the towering flank of the Mark II, snorted at the stink of hot oil and ozone, found the rusted handholds, and pulled myself up—

Bullets *spang!*ed off metal above me. Someone

was trying for me with a slug rifle. The sprained arm hung at my side like a fence-post nailed to my shoulder, but I was hardly aware of the pain now. The hatch stood open half an inch. I grabbed the stiff lever, strained; it gave, swung wide with a squeal. No lights came up to meet me; with the port cracked, they'd burned out long ago. I dropped inside, wriggled through the narrow crawl space into the cockpit. It was smaller than the Mark III—and it was occupied. It was apparent now that the two Bolos had fought to a draw.

In the faint green light from the panel, the dead man crouched over the controls, one dessicated hand in a shrivelled black glove clutching the control bar. He wore a GI weather suit and a white crash helmet, and one foot was twisted nearly backward, caught behind a jack lever. The leg had been broken before he died; he must have jammed the foot and twisted it so that the pain would hold off the sleep that had come at last. I leaned forward to see the face. The blackened and mummified features behind the perspex showed only the familiar anonymity of death, but the name lettered across the helmet was clear enough.

"Hello, Johnny," I said. "Sorry to keep you waiting; I got held up." I wedged myself into the co-pilot's seat, flipped the IR screen switch. The eight-inch monitor panel glowed an eerie green, showed the Mark III trampling through the fence three hundred yards away, moving onto the ramp, dragging a length of rusty chain-link like a bridal train behind it.

I put my hand on the control bar. "I'll take it now, Johnny," I said, and moved the bar. The dead man's hand moved with it, rocking the mummy forward.

I said, "Okay, Johnny, we'll do it together." Maybe I was a little delirious by then.

I hit switches, cancelling the preset response pattern. It had done its job, and now it was time to crank in some human tactics.

My Bolo rocked slightly under a hit, and I heard tread shields drop down. The chair bucked under me, as Mallon bored in, pouring on the fire. Beside me, Johnny nodded patiently. It was old stuff to him. I watched the tracers on the screen. Hosing me down with contact exploders probably gave Mallon a lot of satisfaction, but it couldn't hurt me. It would be a different story when he tired of the game and tried the heavy stuff. But then, maybe the Mark III was as tired as my Mark II.

I thought about places to hide; there weren't any. But I remembered open silos behind me in the dark. It wouldn't do to forget those; but maybe Tobey would, or would with a little encouragement . . .

I threw in the drive, backed away carefully. Mallon's tracers followed for a few yards, then cut off abruptly.

I pivoted, flipped on my polyarcs, raced for the position I had selected near the silos, then swung to face Mallon as he moved toward me. It had been a long time since he had handled the controls of a Bolo; he was rusty, relying on his automatics—and he didn't know his side-scan was out.

I had no heavy artillery, but my pop-guns were OK. I homed my 4mm solid-slug cannon on

Mallon's polyarc, pressed the FIRE button. There was a squawk from my high-velocity-feed magazine. The blue-white light flared yellow and went out. The Bolo defenses could handle anything short of an H-bomb, pick a missile out of the stratosphere a hundred and fifty miles out, devastate a county with one round from its mortars—but my BB gun at point-blank range had poked out its eye.

I switched everything off and sat silent, waiting. Mallon had come to a dead stop. I could picture him staring at the dark screens, slapping levers and cursing. He would be confused, wondering what had happened. With his lights gone, he'd be on radar now—not really sensitive at this range, not too conscious of details like open silo doors.

An amber warning light winked on my panel: Mallon's radar was locked on me. He moved forward again, then stopped; he was having trouble making up his mind about charging in the dark. I flipped a key to drop the padded shock frames in place; Johnny looked relaxed, but I braced myself. Mallon would be getting mad by now.

Crimson danger lights flared on the board, and I rocked under the recoil as my interceptors flashed out to meet Mallon's C-S's and detonate them in incandescent rendezvous over the scarred concrete between us. My screens went white, then dropped back to secondary sensitivity, flashing dim black-and-white. But Mallon couldn't see any better. My ears hummed like trapped hornets; the frame battered at me—

The sudden silence was like a vault door closing. I sagged back, feeling like Quasimodo after a wild ride on the bells. The screens blinked bright again, and I watched the Mark III, sitting motionless now in its near-blindness. On his radar screen I would show as a blurred hill; Mallon would be wondering why I hadn't returned his fire, why I hadn't turned and run, why . . . why . . .

He lurched and started toward me. I waited, then eased back, slowly now, maneuvering meticulously, luring him toward the silos. Unsuspecting, he accelerated, closing in, to come to grips at a range where even the split microsecond response of a Mark II's defenses would be too slow to hold off his fire. I backed across the narrow strip of pavement between the gaping mouths of the empty silos, feeling my way, letting him gain, but not too fast . . .

He knew he had me at his mercy, outgunned and, he thought, outmaneuvered.

Mallon couldn't wait; he opened up, throwing a mixed bombardment from his .9cm's, his infinite repeaters, and his C-S's. I held on, fighting the battering frame. I glanced at Johnny; he was taking it calmly, except that his left hand had broken off at the wrist. The gloved fist was still clamped to the bar while the crumbling, truncated stump poked from his cuff.

I had a few more feet to go, walking the brink, watching my screens; then I was past the yawning pits. Careful, now, careful, I told myself, unnecessarily. Mallon was still coming on. The gap closed: a hundred yards, ninety, eighty. The open silos yawned in Mallon's path now, but he didn't see them. The mighty Bolo came on, guns bellowing in the night, closing for the kill. It eased past the first silo with one tread half over the edge. I waited, decoying him in . . . On the brink of the second fifty-foot-wide, hundred-yard-deep pit dead ahead, the Mark III hesitated, as though sensing danger; then it moved forward that last foot, and I saw it rock forward, dropping its titanic prow, showing its broad back, gouging the blasted pavement as its guns bore on the ground. Great sheets of sparks flew as the treads reversed, too late. The Bolo hung for a moment longer, then majestically slid down like a sinking liner, its guns still firing into the pit like a challenge to Hell, and then it was gone and a dust cloud boiled for a moment, then whipped away as displaced air tornadoed from the open mouth of the silo.

The earth trembled under the impact far below.

I climbed out into a stink of scorched metal and ozone. Over by the fence, all Tobey's army would have seen would have been the Great Troll disappearing like magic. They were busy backing up and turning around and getting the hell out of there. I hiked over to where I'd left Renada, helped her up, told her Tobey's fate. She took it well.

"The Primary Site blockhouse is only a little way," I told her, exaggerating a little. We made it across in slow steps. Inside there'd be warmth, food, and rest. We reached the squat building; now to get inside. But I needn't have worried.

The doors of the Primary Site blockhouse were nine-foot-high, eight-inch-thick panels of solid chromalloy that even a Bolo would have slowed down for, but they slid aside for my electropass like a shower curtain at the YW. We went into a shadowy room where eighty years of silence hung like black crepe on a coffin. The tiled floor was still immaculate, the air fresh; here at the heart of the site, all systems were still go. We went on.

In the central control bunker, nine rows of green lights glowed on the high panel over red letters that spelled out STAND BY FOR MAIN IGNITION. Well, touching off an ion drive wasn't exactly ignition, but the phrase was traditional. A foot to the left, the big white lever stood in the unlocked position, six inches from the outstretched fingertips of the mummified corpse strapped into the controller's chair. The name on his pocket was "MacGregor."

"Commander MacGregor!" Renada exclaimed, delightedly. "I've heard of him!"—as if she were meeting him at a reception. No screams and faints for her.

To the right, a red glow on the monitor panel indicated the lock doors open. It had been close—one second and counting.

"It's awesome," Renada said softly. "I've read about it, but actually to see the technology—" Her voice faltered. "What a waste!" she blurted. "It must have been wonderful to be alive then." She blinked wet eyelashes at me. "And yet you were willing to leave it all—for the Mission."

"So were Don Banner and Johnny Black and the others," I reminded her.

"It's good that it didn't get off," she said. "Suppose they had come back—to this . . . !"

"Let's check out the ship," I suggested. She nodded and sniffed, gave her eyes a final dab.

We rode the service lift down to K level, stepped out onto the steel-railed platform that hugged the sweep of the starship's hull, stepped through into the narrow crew box. To the left were the four sealed covers under which the Primary crew waited: Day, Macy, Cruciani, and Dalton. I went close, read dials. Slender needles trembled minutely to the beating of sluggish hearts. Mac's nap-cans were better than he'd known. The men were alive, after ninety years, and good for another century. But they wouldn't have to wait that long. I didn't hesitate.

I threw in the emergency abort levers, one, two, three, four. It was done.

Suddenly, I was in a panic. Was it too late to abort the abort? Yes, they'd never be able to go back into vital suspension. I'd been thinking about seeing the guys again, all the things we could do, not really facing the fact that without a crew, *Prometheus* would never fly. In a way, I realized, feeling sickish, I felt relieved. The decision was made—but not really, another aspect of my mind jeered. The ship itself was intact, her integrity unviolated, even by Tobey's meddling. She could still lift; we could get up a crew somehow—but the switches were thrown. I felt dazed, disoriented. What was I doing? What *should* I be doing?

Renada looked at me meltingly. She knew what I had done.

"It will take about fifteen minutes for the presequence," I told her, trying to sound brisk. "Then they'll go on manual, and—" The sharp *clack!* from Captain Day's can cut off my little speech. Renada caught my arm. "It's moving!" she whispered. I nodded. We watched the can slide out; the cover cycled open and there was Bob Day, just opening his eyes, which he blinked vigorously. He looked the same as ever; he was always phenomenally quick at recovering.

"Easy, Bob," I said. "Just relax and let the old nervous system come up to revs." His hand was still on the manual override. He relaxed and squinted at us, then opened wide and stared at Renada.

"Whiz," he said, with only a little croak in his voice. He cleared his throat, winced, and tried again. "What's going on? Is there an abort? What's wrong? Did they find the President's plane—or what?"

"Easy, Bob," I repeated. "You're okay. Things aren't good, but there's nothing to worry about. You've been in—"

"What're you doing out, Whiz?" he cut me off. "We were at minus five minutes—are we—are you—?"

"No trouble," I told him. "But there's been a change in procedure."

"Does Mac know that?" He came back fast. By now he was sitting up, feeling for the floor, getting ready to stand.

"Don't be in a hurry, Captain," I told him. "It's been quite a while. You're still at home. The launch was aborted. It's been over ninety years."

His face, already pale, went greenish around the edges. "You're crazy!" he snapped. "All right, that's enough horseplay! Where's Mac? What's going on?"

"There's been a civil collapse," I told him. "No war, an internal breakdown. The launch was aborted, but *Prometheus* is undamaged. I've been out for about two weeks. This is Renada, Don's great-granddaughter. We came here to release you and the others. Banner and Mallon and Johnny Black are dead, and Mac, too—but that's another story. How do you feel?"

He was on his feet, wobbly, just as I had been, and confused, like me, but he was taking it well. But then he'd been Mission Commander. There wasn't much Bob Day couldn't handle.

37

We were in the galley five minutes later, and Day was pitching into some issue grub as if he hadn't eaten for a week. The continuous drip-feed system had been one of the last bugs to be worked out of the life-support system, but it had done its job. Bob hadn't lost more than a couple of pounds, the design figure, and his muscle tone was good, better than mine had been. I knew from my own experience he didn't feel any way you could call good—but he was functioning, and he was eager to do something. I led the way back to Personnel Deck aboard ship.

"It's going to take years, Bob," I told him, trying to give him the news gently. "For ninety years and more, there's been no government, no order, no society."

He interrupted me to say, "What are you talking about? It hasn't been more than a day since I told Ellen—" Renada nodded and shushed him. He got his face back together, and I went on:

"The people have survived, but society didn't. We're culturally back in the Mesolithic, but they do their hunting and gathering in the derelict stores. There are a few pigs and chickens around, but

265

they fend for themselves, and nobody will eat them. No food crops, but there are still some fruit trees around. They think it's unnatural to eat anything that's not in a can—except at the palace; Tobey made sure he had his own food supply, a garden and some meat on the hoof—"

"Hold on," Day held up a hand in protest. "What's this about Tobey Mallon? And where are the big-non-governmental organizations, the Unions, the big corporations, the Red Cross, the civic clubs, the universities? They can't all have reverted to savagery."

"No, most of them disappeared completely," I explained, trying not to sound impatient, "and the brass who survived the initial orgy of looting and paying off grudges were in the same boat as everyone else. No help there." I waited to let that soak in. "We're the only hope," I told him. "We have to bring out Macy and Whop and Joe and use what we have to do what we can."

"What! Abandon the mission?" He threw down his paper napkin and stood, staring down at me.

"Where in hell's Mac?" he yelled. He looked at Renada. "Miss, this is a top secret area. How did you—?"

He swayed, and sat down again fast. "Wait a minute," he growled. "This is one G; I'm still on Earth. Wha—"

I was nodding encouragingly. "That's what I've been trying to tell you, sir," I said, trying not to sound as if I were nagging. "I did some research in the newspaper files; after Air Force One disappeared, the Pentagon got ready for action, but there were riots; the War Riots, they were called.

Mobs yelling for war, other mobs against. The mobs clashed; there was killing, burning, looting on a grand scale; there weren't enough jails. Congress scheduled an—'extra-Constitutional,' they called it—election. Nobody came. Then the tax revolt; nobody paid. The mobs looted the banks and burned all the paper, including the paper money. By the end of the first year, the economy was paralyzed: no government, no food, no clean water, epidemics of everything from AIDS to flu—"

Bob tried to interrupt, but I held up a hand and told him to listen, *then* ask questions. He almost pulled rank, but thought better of it. It's hard to be a martinet in your underwear with a headache.

"What about my crew?" he rasped out. "What about Cruciani and Dalton and Ikey Macy?" He looked around, seeing things for the first time, including the other three sealed cans.

"We'll bring them out next," I said. That shook him; he stood up and pushed his face at me.

"Who in hell authorized *you* to cancel *Prometheus*, Mister?" he not-quite-yelled.

"Nobody, Captain," I told him, also not quite yelling. "They're all dead except us, get it? It's been a long time. A really long time. Now, me and you, Bob; the human race needs us. So calm down and let's start talking sense about what has to be done."

He tried to push me aside and almost fell over backwards. That made him curse, then apologize to Renada. "Weak as a damned kitten," he said to himself, aloud. "What in hell—"

"Perhaps, Captain Day," Renada spoke up, "it would be best to listen to what Commander Jackson is telling you—what *I'm* telling you. Your world no longer exists. There's no NASA, no Nice Day, no electricity, no regulations."

" 'No war,' you said?" he croaked, his eyes appealing for help.

"Internal collapse," I told him. "The same thing happened in Redland: in fact, they had their revolution a few hours before the EC election farce. And Japan and WEU, as far as I could determine from the ninety-year-old newspapers."

"You're crazy!" Bob told me, with both hands on top of his head as if to hold it in place. It was more of a plea than a protest.

"Ninety years?" he uttered the words hesitantly. "That means Ellen, and little Bobby and—"

I nodded, trying to ease the blow. "They had their lives," I reminded him. Briefly I thought of Jeannie. I hoped she was still all right, that Mallon's Greenbacks hadn't raided.

38

A couple of hours later, Bob and Renada and I were helping Whop Cruciani and Macy into the galley. They were shaky and weak, as expected, but basically all right. When Renada protested Bob's calling Whop "Whop," I explained that he got the nickname on Day One of our pre-orientation when he looked at the centrifuge trainer, shook his head and commented, "If that chest-strap lets go, you'll fly sixty feet and"—he skipped one palm across the other—"*whop!* against the concrete!"

We gave them the story in small doses, evoking protests about everything from aborting the mission to missing the Dodgers game. But before long they accepted the strange fact that they weren't on an unknown planet, a few million miles from home, but were in the ruins of home itself.

"What we have to do," Whop stated seriously, "is get this mess organized. Sounds like Tobey's palace is a start. We'll recruit enough good people—"

"Seems like there aren't any good people," Ike Macy contributed.

"I meant healthy ones," Whop amended, "and we'll teach them some discipline—"

"Betsy can help with that," I pointed out. "The

Grand Army can be the nucleus of an effective force."

"Sure," Whop agreed. "From what you said, they'll be a good start."

"Then," Bob added, "we carry out a systematic salvage operation, and stockpile everything useful, and set up a rationing system."

The other fellows were full of ideas, too, eager to get started. I realized they all assumed the mission was scratched. But—I decided to defer that decision—it wasn't too late to get the crew back aboard and go . . .

"We've got pigs and chickens," I contributed. "All we need to do is round them up and build pens and get people used to the idea food doesn't have to come out of a can. Plenty of cattle, too," I mused. "They've reverted to the aurochs type, *Bos primigenius*, but our ancestors tamed them and so can we."

"I always liked gardening," Cruciani put in. "I'll bet we can find enough crop plants growing wild to start a few farms."

The boys were full of ideas for a good couple of hours; then they began to get sleepy; it was time for a good rest. After ninety-odd years in a can, you might think that was unnecessary, but drug-induced coma isn't the same thing thing as real sleep, with dreaming. We got them tucked in in the standby quarters, and Renada and I looked at each other.

"They're wonderful men," she said. "And you, too, Commander Jackson. You especially," she added. "It's going to be wonderful," she dreamed on. "Imagine! With the magic back—the electricity, I mean—"

"It's magic, kid. If you don't think so," I told my biographers, "try doing without it."

"If Tobey's arrangements work," Renada said doubtfully.

"All the guys agree they will," I reminded her. "All we have to do is throw the big switch to find out. Let's go."

39

We left the ship, walking through the Primary control area. Back in the control bunker, the monitor panel still showed ALL CLEAR FOR LAUNCH. I looked at Mallon's rewired COMMIT lever. Everything was set now; if I threw it, *Prometheus* would wait in her berth for eternity, but the lights in the ruined houses would go on again. I was still thinking it over. Tobey's power plant would be ready to go—except for the special final switch he'd rigged back in the palace to keep control as his personal prerogative. If I didn't throw it, and got the crew suited up again instead, the hiatus in human cultural evolution would go on—perhaps for centuries —before mankind reattained a level comparable to what we'd had . . .

Even after talking it over with the crew, who didn't seem much interested, I still wasn't quite ready to be the one to give the *coup de grace* to *Prometheus*. I stood in front of that damned switch for an hour.

Renada came up beside me. She spoke softly. "What will you do now?" she asked me, almost diffidently.

"You mean 'we,' don't you?" I suggested. "I'm no baron, remember, kid."

She backed away as if uncertain what to say. "Come on, Ren," I urged. "Relax. His Excellency's gone. It's up to us, now."

"What will you do now?" she repeated.

"We'd better not waste any time," I said. "Even after eighty years—or was it ninety? I'll have to work it out precisely some day—the countdown's not to be unnecessarily delayed."

"What do you mean?" Her voice was strained.

"This is launch day, kid," I told her, feeling pretty proud of my decision. But she didn't break into that beautiful smile. She shook her head.

"No, Jackson," she said. "You *can't*. It would be *wrong*, don't you see that?" She came over and grabbed my arm with both hands and looked at my face as if searching for a ray of hope.

" 'Wrong'?" I echoed. "After all these years and all the dedication and millions we poured into *Prometheus*? Wrong? I don't understand you."

"Tobey was right about one thing," Renada said steadily. "The ship is a treasure house of technology and supplies. And the men—their knowledge —we need them! The human *race* needs them. We can't send it all off on a pointless expedition. 'Years,' you say? No, eons, Jackson: since the first living cell appeared, all those millions of years of evolution—all wasted, if humanity dies now. But we have the power to save it all." She paused, then said steadily, "The stars must wait."

"You're talking about human evolution," I reminded her, "life crawling out of the sea and all the rest. Fine. The next step is to jump off the home planet. It's our destiny that's waiting, Renada, I never told you, but part of the mission was to establish a stockpile of sperm and ova to be maintained on Callisto indefinitely in cryogenic storage, both animal and human. It's possible that with the right new crew we could set up a permanent, *viable* colony." I didn't add that the chances were starvation slim, but she could see it in my face.

"Later," she suggested. "When we've recovered. Perhaps in a thousand years they can plan the trip again."

"Have you even considered," I asked her, "that a thousand years from now—or from any date to a millennium later—every human alive will be a descendent of everyone alive at the earlier date? In this case, us, as well as all those folks out there." I tilted my head to indicate the barbarians rooting in the ruins of a civilization. "Think about it: every person has to have over ten to the twelfth *direct* ancestors a thousand years before. And what's the population today? Maybe a few million, including us; so everyone alive in a thousand years will be our direct descendants via over a hundred million lines of descent. You want me to rob them— our own umpteen-great-grandkids—of their heritage?"

"No, Jackson," she said steadily. "I want to *give* it to them. There's only one way. We have to cannibalize your precious *Prometheus*." Her voice was cold, but it quavered on the last word.

"Let's go back aboard and take a closer look," I suggested. "The discussion may be academic. Tobey's power plant scheme may have already damaged her beyond repair after all. He said not, but then he no longer cared."

She grabbed up her fur wrap and winced pulling it on; her arm was worse than she'd let on.

"Me, destroy *Prometheus*?" I was muttering to myself, trying the idea on for size. I remembered Frank and Finette, struggling in their makeshift Spittle, getting set for another winter. Well, maybe I could at least consider it. I started to say, "The decision is go," but somehow, without intending to, I reached out and threw the switch instead. Now when the coil was energized, instead of throwing the great ship clear of earth, it would pour a torrent of energy into the power grid.

Renada hugged me. "It was the only right thing to do, Jackson," she assured me. "After all, *Prometheus* isn't our private property. It really belongs to all of *them*." She motioned with her lovely head to indicate all the people out there, still camping in the decaying ruins. "This is the wrong time to spend their last life's-blood on a one-chance-in-a-million adventure. Bob Day would agree with me, I know. And the others, too."

That was something else I'd think about later, when I had to.

I touched her hand and said, "Let's go back to the Hilton and work out our plans. We have to get hold of Colonel Powell and prepare Tobey's army for the transition."

"They'll do whatever you say," she told me. "They're not really such bad fellows, most of them— and there are Tobey's hostages to release and send back with a peace offer—and the women and kids, too."

Outside in the darkness the Bolo waited. I helped Renada in, then climbed to a perch in the open conning tower twenty feet above the broken pavement, and we moved off toward the east where sunrise colors picked out the high towers of the palace.

40

After we closed the big circuit breaker in Tobey's inner sanctum, we went out on the balcony. It was up to Tobey's rerigged automatics now.

Finally we were leaning on the balcony rail, looking out across the valley and the town to the misty plain under which *Prometheus* waited. Throwing the big switch hadn't been as traumatic as I'd expected. The fifteen-second fire-up sequence seemed to go on and on. Had he made a mistake, destroyed the mechanism?

"There's something happening now," Renada said, and handed me the binoculars; I watched as the silo cover rolled back.

"There's smoke," Renada said.

"Don't worry; just cooling gases being vented off." I looked at my watch. "Another minute or two and we'll know just what kind of engineer Tobey was."

"And if it was bad?" Renada voiced the question that hung over us all.

"We'll never know it," I told her. "We'll be part of the fireball within a millisecond . . ."

"And if it *doesn't* blow," Renada said, "what then?"

"We'll be busy trying to put together a world for our kids to grow up in. I don't think we'll be bored."

"Look!" Renada gripped my arm.

On the scraped-bare rectangle of the site, smoke/dust/steam was venting from the Primary silo like a rumbling volcano. The polyarcs around the site winked on, a jeweled necklace around the hopes of mankind. Behind me I heard the hum of ion-motors starting up and hot air wafted from the cooling tower beside us. Then, all across the ruined town, and here and there in the once-verdant valley, small, bright lights sprang up, dissipating the long darkness. Renada moved into my arms.

"About those kids of ours," she murmured.

Postscript

Captain Bob Day took charge of inventory and assigned jobs to the rest of us without asking anybody's permission. For the present, we couldn't touch Philly itself: too much fear of the Noocler. We'd get to it later, after the education classes.

We found an amazing amount of dehydrated and irradiated foods; the collapse had happened too fast for any really organized looting of the stock-piles. We were lucky; the unexpected reactivation of electric service hadn't started any fires or any other disasters except for a few minor shocks—both physical, when a few curious folks poked metal into the live outlets when the lights came on, and psychological, when familiar inert objects abruptly began to hum and rotate. A few TVs started blasting a roar of white sound and light; folks thought it was the Noocler for sure. But they were impressed with our *mana* when we sent in a party of Palace-trained men to help explain the care and feeding of AC systems and household appliances. The people in general were delighted, with the lighting especially, and were soon using electric hand tools and hotplates as if they'd always had them. And there were no meter-readers; never again.

The first distribution of food had gone off pretty well, once we succeeded in convincing the recipients of two things: first, that our people weren't there to attack; *and* that although they were giving away food, they weren't victims to be stoned, beaten, or tied up and dragged across the ground. I don't know which idea they clung to most tenaciously, but by the fifth day, we had orderly lines waiting, if not patiently, at least resignedly, for their handouts.

That accomplished, the time was right to start getting them used to the idea of eating something that didn't come out of a can. Simple gardening was first, using the hardy surviving feral descendents of our old domesticated tomatoes, potatoes, and beans. We kept finding more and more kinds of squash, nuts, and berries, and lots of edible cabbage variants—including brussels sprouts the size of apples, giant broccoli, and many forms of a new cabbage we called "salad stalks" that was good raw, like celery.

Then there were the grains, of course. We were able to plow and plant some respectable acreage after the third year. Those scrub pigs were plenty mean, but we ate the adults and tamed the piglets, and gradually people got used to them, especially after they tasted bacon and pork chops for the first time. (We did have a little trouble disabusing their minds of the swine-god Basser-Sumbish, but taste goes a long way.)

We didn't bother with the horses. The tractors would be ready soon enough, but the bovines took ten years before the resurgent aurochs genes had been bred down enough to make it practical to milk a cow. The fowls were a lot easier, of course, once they were caught and penned up.

The job of overhauling and extending the existing water and energy distribution systems was a formidable one, but we started in. Road repair had to wait, although we soon had a sizable fleet of operating vehicles. We were able to rehabilitate a surprisingly high percentage of the still-standing structures, mainly by improvising new roofs, at least enough to keep the weather out, using hand-hewn timbers from the resurgent forests of pine and oak. There was an adequate stockpile of roofing tiles, asphalt paper, and synthetic shingles to get almost everyone in out of the increasingly mild weather, the latter due to the once-dreaded greenhouse effect.

There weren't any laws yet, or new TV shows, but after a few years my grandson Timmy was living almost as well as the average citizen of Nice Day had, a hundred years before, and nobody was talking about war, race-relations (what's that?), or overpopulation.

We made contact with Jersey and Dee-Cee and entered into negotiations. By logic, reason, patience, a few truckloads of fresh food, and one Bolo Mark II, we persuaded them to suspend hostilities and join in the restoration effort.

I look forward to the future, and hardly ever think of *Prometheus*.

ANNE McCAFFREY
ELIZABETH MOON

Sassinak was twelve when the raiders came. That made her just the right age: old enough to be used, young enough to be broken. Or so the slavers thought. But Sassy turned out to be a little different from your typical slave girl. Maybe it was her unusual physical strength. Maybe it was her friendship with the captured Fleet crewman. Maybe it was her spirit. Whatever it was, it wouldn't let her resign herself to the life of a slave. She bided her time, watched for her moment. Finally it came, and she escaped. But that was only the beginning for Sassinak. Now she's a Fleet captain with a pirate-chasing ship of her own, and only one regret in her life: not enough pirates.

SASSINAK
You're going to love her!

Coming in March, from
BAEN BOOKS